DONOVAN'S
BRAIN

DONOVAN'S BRAIN

CURT SIODMAK

CARROLL & GRAF PUBLISHERS, INC.
New York

Dedication: To Henrietta

First Carroll & Graf edition 1985

Carroll & Graf Publishers, Inc.
260 Fifth Avenue
New York, NY 10001

ISBN: 0-88184-154-4

Manufactured in the United States of America.

SEPTEMBER 13

TODAY a Mexican organ-grinder passed through Washington Junction. He carried a small Capuchin monkey which looked like a wizened old man. The animal was sick, dying of tuberculosis. Its moth-eaten fur was tawny olive, greasy, and full of hairless patches.

I offered three dollars for the monkey, and the Mexican was eager to sell. Tuttle, the drugstore-owner, wanted to keep me from buying it, but he was afraid to interfere lest I stop patronizing his place and make my purchases in Konapah or Phoenix.

I wrapped the flea-ridden Capuchin in my coat and carried it home. It shivered in spite of the burning heat, but when I held it closer, it bit me.

The animal trembled with fear as we entered my laboratory. I chained it to the leg of the work table, then washed my wound thoroughly with disinfectant. After that, I fed the creature some raw eggs and talked to it. It calmed down —till I tried to pet it, then it bit me again.

Franklin, my colored man, brought me a cardboard box which he had half-filled with hemp. The hemp would smother the fleas, he explained. My monkey nimbly hopped into the box and hid there. When I paid it no further attention, it soon fell asleep. I studied its almost hairless face, its head covered with short fur that resembled the cowl of a Capuchin monk. The animal was breathing with difficulty and I was afraid it might not live through the night.

SEPTEMBER 14

THE monkey was still alive this morning and screamed hysterically when I tried to grab it. But after I fed it bananas and raw egg again, it let me pet its head a moment. I had to make it trust me completely. Fear causes an excess secretion of adrenalin, resulting in an abnormal condition of the blood stream; this would throw off my observations.

This afternoon, the Capuchin put its long arms around my chest and pressed its face against my shoulder, in perfect confidence. I stroked it slowly, and it uttered small whimpers of content. I tried its pulse, which was away above normal.

When it began to sleep in my arms, I stabbed it between the occipital bone and the first cervical vertebra. It died instantly.

SEPTEMBER 15

AT three o'clock this afternoon Dr. Schratt came from Konapah to visit me. Though I often do not see him for weeks at a time, we communicate freely by phone and letter. He is very interested in my work but, as he watches my experiments, he cannot hide his misgivings. He does not conceal his satisfaction when he sees me failing in an experiment. His soul is torn between a scientific compulsion (which is also mine), and a pusillanimous reaction against what he calls: "invading God's own hemisphere."

Schratt has lived in Konapah for more than thirty years. The heat has dried up his energies. He has become as superstitious as the Indians of his district. If his medical ethics permitted, he would prescribe snake charms and powdered toads for his patients.

He is official physician for the emergency landing field at Konapah, and the small sum paid him by the airline keeps him from starving. There is not very much business around here to feed a country doctor. The few white people go to the hospital in Phoenix when they are ill; the Indians only call a white doctor when all the mystic charms have failed and the patient is dying.

Schratt once had the makings of a Pasteur or a Robert Koch. Half drowned in cheap tequila now, he has lost the ability to concentrate. But still sometimes a flash of genius illuminates the twilight of his consciousness. Afraid of that lightning-flash of vision, he deliberately withdraws into the haze of his slowly simmering life.

He watched me this afternoon with fatherly hatred. If he could forbid me to do what I am doing, he would. But forgotten wishes and dreams sometimes echo in the ruins of his wretched life. His antagonism to me and my work is pure manifestation of his regret that he has betrayed his own genius.

Sitting in a deep chair near the fireplace, he smoked his pipe nervously. How he can stand the desert heat in that thick old coat he brought from Europe forty years ago I shall never know. Maybe it is the only one he has.

I am quite sure that each time he leaves me he takes an oath never to see me again. But every few days my telephone rings and his hoarse, tired voice asks for me—or his aged Ford stops, boiling, in front of my house.

I had dissected the monkey's carcass. The lungs were infected with tuberculosis, which had also attacked the kidneys. But the brain was in good shape. To preserve it, I placed it in an artificial respiratory.

I fixed rubber arteries to the vertebral and internal carotid arteries of the brain, and the blood substance, forced by a small pump, streamed through the circle of Willis to supply the brain. It flowed out through the corresponding veins on both sides and passed through glass tubes which I had irradiated with ultraviolet.

The strength and frequency of the infinitesimal electric charges the brain was producing were easy to measure. The electroencephalograms marked their slow, trembling curves on the paper strip which continuously flowed from the wave-recording machine.

I was very eager to hear Schratt's comment on my success, but he only stared, irritated, at the wavering line which scrawled an irregular frieze pattern on the paper strip.

He lifted his thick brown fingers and touched once the glass in which the brain was floating. Immediately, disturbed, the brain-waves altered, rose and fell with ever increasing rapidity. The detached organ was reacting to an external stimulus!

"It feels—it *thinks!*" Schratt said. When he turned around I saw the spark in his eyes I had eagerly expected.

But Schratt sat down heavily. As he thought of what he had seen, he grew pale under the coarse, brownish skin that loosely covered his drink-sodden face.

"You're the godfather of this phenomenon," I said to cheer him up, in spite of knowing he could not be flattered.

I don't want any part of anything you are doing, Patrick," he answered. "You, with your mechanistic physiology, reduce life to physical chemistry! This brain may still be able to feel pain; it may suffer, though bodyless, eyeless, and deprived of any organ to express its feeling. It may be writhing in agony!"

"We know that the brain itself is *in*sensitive," I answered quietly. To please him I added: "At least we *believe* we know that!"

"You have put it in a nutshell," Schratt answered. I perceived that he was trembling; the success of my experiment had unnerved him. "You believe and acknowledge only what you are able to observe and measure. You recklessly push through to your discoveries with no thought of the consequences."

I had heard him express this view before.

"I only try to cultivate living tissues outside the body," I patiently answered. "You must agree, in spite of your abhorrence of everything concerned in the progress of science, that my experiment is a big step forward. You told me the fragility of nervous substance is too great to be studied in the living state. But I have done it!"

I touched the glass which contained the Capuchin's brain,

and the encephalograph at once registered the reaction of the irritated tissues.

I watched Schratt closely. I wanted to have from him again that admixture of genius which fertilized my researches. But Schratt's expression was blank and remote.

"You're synthetic and concise," he finally said unhappily. "There's no human emotion left in you. Your passion for observation and your mathematical precision have killed it, Patrick. Your intelligence is crippled by a profound inability to understand life. I am convinced that life is a synthesis of love and hatred, ambition and aimlessness, vanity and kindness. When you can manufacture kindness in a test tube, I'll be back."

He walked slowly and forlornly to the door, as always when he had made up his mind to break with me. But in the doorway he turned and added in a trembling voice: "Do me a favor, Patrick! Shut off the pump. Let that poor thing in there die!"

SEPTEMBER 16

AFTER midnight the deflections of the encephalograph ceased, and the monkey's brain died.

The telephone in the living-room rang at three in the morning, while I was still working in the laboratory. I heard the bell shrill faintly again and again. Janice had gone to bed hours ago, after bringing me some supper on a tray.

Obviously she had taken a sleeping draught, or the bell's persistent ringing would have wakened her. Franklin, who slept in the cottage in the back, would never get up.

When I finally took down the receiver, I heard Ranger White's excited voice. A plane had crashed near his station.

"I can't reach Konapah!" White shouted as if he had to talk to me across the distance without the help of a telephone. "Old Doc Schratt is drunk again."

He began to swear, out of control of himself—a man alone in a blockhouse on top of a mountain, eight hard miles from the nearest dwelling, with a crashed plane close to him.

He had tried Schratt for ten minutes before he switched the call to me. He had only two lines to choose from—Schratt's and mine. The telephone operator leaves these connections open all night in case of emergencies.

I calmed White down and promised speedy help.

Finally I got Schratt on the phone. He could hardly talk or even understand what I was telling him. I repeated the information again and again.

"I can't get up there!" he whined when my words had penetrated his tequila-fogged brain. "I can't. I'm an old man. I can't sit on a horse for hours. I've got a bad heart!"

He was deadly afraid of losing his job, but the alcohol had paralyzed him.

"All right, I'll take over for you," I said. "Meet me at my house tonight."

"At your house tonight, Patrick," he repeated plaintively. "Thanks, Patrick. Thanks. . . ."

To wake Franklin from his sleep was a job. I ordered him to call the neighbors and to get me some help. Then I went back to the laboratory and packed my bag with all the instruments and medication I thought I would need. When I looked up, Janice stood in the door.

She had put on her morning gown and with thin fingers was trying to fasten the belt at her waist. Her eyes were tired and dull. She had drugged herself. I saw that at once.

She cannot bear the climate, the heat of the parched desert, the sudden sandstorms, the stale water that is pumped through miles of hot pipelines. She was withering away slowly, desiccating. I had told her often enough to leave Washington Junction. She should live in New England, where she was born. But she will not leave me.

"Emergency?" she asked, pulling herself together, battling the drug.

I told her about the plane and White's call.

"Let me go with you," she asked, but her tongue was thick. "I can help. . . ."

She was suddenly awake, restless. I knew she only wanted to be with me, close to me, and the crash was a pretext.

"No," I said, "you're not fit for the trip. Go to bed."

I realized I had not talked to her for weeks. Her shadow was always behind me—my food in my room at the right moment, the house cleaned noiselessly, and she never bothered me with questions. She was waiting for me to call her, but I had forgotten her shadowy existence.

The men arrived with the horses and mules. We went up the mountain trail.

OUR horses had climbed for three hours when we came to White's ranger station. It is a blockhouse of heavy timbers and a tower from which the observer has the wide view over the mountains. White's job is to keep lookout for fires and see that the batteries for the revolving lights are charged properly. The beacons are landmarks for planes flying to the north and west.

White is a man of about fifty. He lives with only his dog in this lonely place. To him even the few inhabitants of Washington Junction are an unbearable crowd. Now, for the first time, I found him wanting to see someone, anyone. His weather-browned face looked livid.

"Glad you came," he said, helping me from my horse.

As he led me to the plane, he added: "It's a goddam mess!"

There was not much left of the ship. The impact of the crash had disintegrated the wings, cabin, and fuselage. Pieces of the plane were scattered over a wide area. It looked as if the pilot had misjudged the height of the mountain.

"It caught fire, but I got it out," White said, and pointed at a still smoldering patch where the blackened gas tank had burst inside out.

"I hope they're still alive." White had done an efficient job in spite of his shock.

He had carried the two survivors into the shade under a tree. One was a young man, the other an older man whose face seemed familiar. Both were still breathing. The young one had his eyes open, but he did not see me. He was semiconscious and his teeth were embedded in his lower lip. A trickle of blood ran down his chin.

I gave him a shot of morphine and turned to the other

man. This one had compound fracture of both legs. White had twisted a tourniquet above each of the man's knees to keep him from bleeding to death.

Tuttle and Phillips approached, but stopped a few yards from the injured men. I did not see Matthews, the third man. He had told me on the way up he could not stand the sight of blood.

Tuttle said: "There're two more guys over there, but they are dead!"

I turned in the indicated direction and saw a propeller buried in the ground, with a part of the motor still attached.

"Their heads are off." Phillip's voice was so low I could not understand him at first.

White had found four bodies. The plane, though powerful, was too small to have carried more.

I ordered White and Phillips to take the older man to the blockhouse. I examined the young man where he lay. His chest was crushed and both arms broken. I told Tuttle to cut four straight branches from the tree.

The man was conscious but could not talk. The morphine had lessened his pain; he was perspiring profusely. His pulse was close to a hundred and ten.

"Take it easy, try to doze off," I told him. "Don't fight. You'll be all right."

He seemed to understand and tried to answer. But the drug was already taking effect, closing his eyes.

I moved his arms carefully across his chest, and padding with bandages the four branches Tuttle had brought me, I laid them against both sides of the humerus and tied them securely at wrist and elbow. I gave the man a second injection to keep him asleep until we got him to the hospital and ordered Tuttle to take him down to Washington Junction, where he would meet the ambulance.

Tuttle called Phillips and they tied the unconscious man on a stretcher. I went back to the house without waiting for them to leave.

White had placed the old man on a table. He was beginning to stir and groan as I loosened the tourniquets from around his legs, which were swelling rapidly.

"They will have to be amputated," I said to White, "or he will die in a few hours."

12

White turned his livid face toward me and nodded. He grinned in an effort to control himself, but I was afraid he would never stick it through.

Now I regretted not having brought Janice. Matthews, the grocer, the only other helper I had still with me, was outside being sick. He had never seen broken bones and mangled bodies before. I talked to him, but he was no help.

I gave White a bromide to calm him down. He became very efficient, carried out all my orders with speed and precision. But he could not stop talking. I let him talk, for it seemed to relieve him. He kept explaining just what had happened.

He had heard the ship cruising overhead soon after midnight. It seemed to have lost its bearings. The beacons were all in working order, but the clouds were unusually thick. White was at a loss to know what plane it was. The commercial from Los Angeles had already passed, and no other information had come from Konapah.

White talked in a staccato voice while he gathered fresh bed linen and white shirts from a drawer. He fired the kitchen stove and put water on to heat, efficient but mechanical. I scrubbed the kitchen table with green soap, which he fortunately had in the house.

White's voice while he moved quietly about was feverish. He had lived at the station eight years. There had never been an accident or irregularity. Once a few trout fisherman stole gasoline from one of the beacons for their stove. That is a Federal offense, but White had not bothered reporting it.

He felt strangely responsible and obsessed by the idea that he might be accused of negligence. He tried to drown his guilt in a torrent of explanations. He took it as a personal misfortune that the crash had occurred near his station.

The water was boiling and I sterilized the instruments. Infection can follow even the most rigid asepsis and his dusty kitchen for an operating theater hardly gave the man on the table a sporting chance. For a minute I considered not operating at all and letting fate decide.

I stepped closer to the man and studied his face. These features were somehow familiar, the thin colorless mouth,

13

the high cheek bones, the short nose, the prominent forehead. Even the scar which ran from the left ear to the tip of the chin seemed known to me.

White had cut the man's coat from him and thrown it on a chair. I took the wallet from the breast pocket. Blood had soaked it and glued the sheaf of big bills together. The man carried a fortune with him! The wallet was old and worn and stamped with the initials W.H.D. Warren Horace Donovan!

Now that I knew who he was I had to save his life. This man was too important. In a few hours dozens of specialists would be poking their noses into this case and if I did not get him down alive I would be accused of negligence. I had to make a clean job of it.

I did not tell White who the man on his kitchen table was. If I had, he would have been too awed and excited to help me.

After cutting away Donovan's trousers and underwear, I injected a spinal anæsthetic between the third and fourth lumbar vertebræ. If the man became conscious now, he would feel no pain.

His respirations were irregular, and I lowered his head by shoving a couple of books under the back legs of the table. The blood pressure was falling alarmingly. I gave Donovan a half cc. of 1-1000 adrenalin intravenously. The pressure rose again. I began the amputation and finished it in less than an hour.

I was obliged to cut through the femur, because the femur bones had suffered multiple fractures and the arteries were severed. A steady stream of arterial blood gushed forth as soon as the tourniquets were loosened. His toes were ice-cold and clammy. Nobody could have saved Donovan's legs. And all the time I was operating I was aware of the futility of my endeavor.

The sun stood high when we tied him to the stretcher to take him down the trail. We fastened the litter between two horses, lowering the rear to carry the body in a fairly level position. The tedious descent began.

I left White behind. Matthews had recovered from the shock and seemed ashamed of his weakness and desertion.

He wanted to make good now and walked beside the stretcher, letting me ride the horse.

Every few minutes we had to stop to take Donovan's pulse. It was around one hundred and forty and very weak. I gave him one cc. of 1-1000 adrenalin intravenously.

When we were two hours on our way, Donovan stopped breathing. I had to pull his tongue forward and administer some oxygen which I carried with me in a small steel flask. He needed an intravenous injection of Coramine, but I did not have it.

I had not slept for two days and I could feel I was close to the end of my resistance. A few times the trail blurred before my eyes. I had to hold tight to the neck of the horse.

The sun seemed to stand still in the sky and the heat became unbearable as we trailed down the pass. Once the horses shied, but Matthews caught the reins in time to keep them from bolting. A rattlesnake was sunning itself across the path. While I held the excited horses, Matthews killed it with a club. Then he threw the crushed body as far as he could, but the dead snake caught in the branches of a tree and we had a bad time leading the horses past. This was torture, climbing downhill with a dying man strung between the horses.

When we finally heard voices hailing us, we stopped at once and sat down, exhausted.

Four men came up the trail to meet us. Schratt had phoned to Phoenix, and the hospital had sent an ambulance. But Schratt had declined the assistance of a doctor from Phoenix. It was his job to take care of these injured. He was sticking to his job, and I was doing it!

Phoenix was still unaware that the plane which had crashed was Warren Horace Donovan's; otherwise all the ethics of the medical profession would not have kept the hospital from sending every available specialist up the mountain to save W. H. Donovan's life!

15

JUST before we got to Washington Junction, Donovan reached a crisis. His strong heart had delayed the coma, but it was too late now to send him on to Phoenix. He could not have arrived alive.

I had him carried into my laboratory and put on the operating table. The men looked around curiously. They had not expected such an elaborate lay-out. None of them knew my name or anything about me. But people who live in the desert are not very curious or talkative. The heat which thins the blood makes the brain sluggish, and no one thinks more than is necessary for the primitive functions of life. I lived secludedly; nobody asked what I was doing. The desert is full of anchorites and lonely people with strange habits.

I sent the men away, then changed to a clean shirt which Janice had left in the laboratory. I found iced coffee on my desk and some food. She was silently waiting in her room for me to call her. The accident had interrupted the monotonous routine of our days and she was hoping I would want to talk to her.

I examined the dying man. His pulse was rapid and his heart-sounds so weak I could hardly hear them with my stethoscope.

I called Janice.

"Where is Schratt?" I asked. I could see she had not slept, waiting for me to return.

"He took the other man to Phoenix," she answered.

"Call up the hospital and tell him to get over here right away. Then come and help me."

She ran out of the room to obey my order.

I had to come to a decision. I had to make up my mind now. At once! Before it was too late. I did not feel exhausted any more. The opportunity was unprecedented. Too tremendous. This man was dying, but his brain was still alive. It was an extraordinary brain, the dome large and of perfect shape, the skull broad, the forehead wide.

16

I tested its reactions with the encephalograph. It showed strong delta deflections.

An animal's brain has weak reactions and very little resistance. An animal gives up when it is going to die. The brain is a minor organ of its body, less important than the weapons of defense. But the man on my table had exercised his brain all his life, trained it, strengthened it. Here was the perfect specimen a scientist might wish for!

If only Schratt were here!

Donovan's skull was nearly hairless. That made it easier. He was in a coma; it was not necessary to use an anæsthetic.

I switched on the sterilizer and put in a surgical scalpel and a Gigli saw.

When the instruments were ready, I picked out the scalpel and made a semicircular incision in the skin just above the right ear, continuing the incision around the back of the head to the upper surface of the left ear. I pulled the scalpel forward until it completely exposed the top of the calvarium. There was very little bleeding from the exposed surfaces.

Taking the Gigli saw, I made an incision in the bony vault completely around the skull. To leave the brain uninjured, I was very careful not to cut through the dura mater. I then lifted off the entire top of the cranial vault *in toto*.

The glistening surface of the dura mater was still warm to my finger's touch.

I made the same semicircular incision in the dura mater that I had in the outer skin.

I pulled the dura forward, and there lay exposed Donovan's brain!

Donovan's breathing stopped; white asphyxia due to cardiac failure began. There was no time to apply stimulants. That would have taken precious minutes. I had to open his brain while he was still alive. I had made that mistake before with the Capuchin, and I could not take any risk now.

I heard Janice at the phone talking to Phoenix. Schratt was on his way back. She repeated the information loudly so I could hear.

If Schratt's Ford didn't break down!

Janice came in. She stopped, seeing me at work over the body.

"Come here," I ordered gruffly. I wanted to give her no time to think. She had studied medicine to please me and have the chance to be closer to me. Concentrated, cool, precise even in emergencies, she was an ideal nurse. But, like Schratt, she deeply resented the work I was doing, for it took me away from her and she was jealous. I was married to my apparatus and scalpels.

"The Gigli saw! Quick!" I said. I stretched out my hand without looking at her. She hesitated, standing there in the doorway. Then I heard her move. She stepped close behind my shoulder and passed me the instrument. I pressed the Gigli saw to the occipital bone. I was so concentrated on my work I did not hear Schratt enter.

Finally I felt someone watching me. Schratt was standing two yards behind me, staring. His face twisting, he battled with himself, undecided whether to run away or come to my assistance, but finally he overcame the shock of seeing me steal a man's brain.

I lifted up the cranium, severed it by cutting the medulla oblongata just above the foramen magnum.

"We would like to be alone, Janice," I said.

She left at once, relieved to go, I felt, and for a second I regretted having called her to help me. I did not want witnesses!

"Put on those gloves and a smock," I said to Schratt, while I loosened the frontal gyrus with a blunt dissector, carefully feeling my way not to injure the eyes.

Schratt impulsively hid his face in his hands and stood motionless for seconds. When he uncovered his face again, his expression had changed. He had known what I was going to do as soon as he entered the laboratory. I was violating his creed and ethics, but he did not refuse to help me, though I had no power to coerce him.

The frustrated potential Pasteur had broken through and Schratt's vocation was stronger than his conscience. I knew that afterward he would have pangs of remorse, fits of repentance he would try to drown in tequila. He knew it too, but he helped me.

He stepped over to the table and pulled on the gloves. Without waiting to put on a smock, he grabbed the knife.

His hands, heavy and coarse-fingered, became subtle. He worked with great speed.

"I'll have to cut here," he muttered, and as I nodded he severed the medulla oblongata.

I took blood serum from the heater, affixed the rubber tube to the rotary pump, and turned on the ultraviolet lights.

"Ready?" Schratt asked.

I nodded, took a steaming towel from the sterilizer, and held it over the brain which Schratt was lifting out of the lower cranium. He carried it over to the glass bowl and submerged it in the serum, fastened the rubber tubes to the vertebral and internal carotid arteries, and set the pump in motion.

"Better hurry," Schratt said, pulling off his gloves. "They may come for the body any minute." His face suddenly looked gray and shriveled. He nodded toward the body. "Better get him in shape. Stuff some cotton in the skull or the eyes might fall in."

I filled the skull cavity with cotton bandages and replaced the cranium, taping it with adhesive. I pulled the scalp back over the calvarium, then I bandaged the head carefully and had foresight enough to soak a few drops of Donovan's blood into the bandages as if a wound from the accident had bled through.

I eagerly turned to see if the brain was still alive, but Schratt stopped me.

"We have done all we can," he said. "Let's get the body out of here. You wouldn't want them to see *that*?" He indicated the brain with a jerky movement of his head. "If we get the body out into the sun, it will decompose fast. I don't want an autopsy."

Excitement had fuddled my judgment, and I submitted to Schratt. But he did not seem to enjoy his new authority.

For years Schratt had been inhibited in my presence, I knew that. He had lost his own ambition and drive, and he envied me my persistence in carrying through the researches. But now, though he had the upper hand at last, he did not take advantage of me. Cowardly he walked out on his opportunity to avenge himself for the humiliations I had involuntarily inflicted upon him through all these years.

We put Donovan's body on a stretcher, covered it with a

sheet, and carried it outside. The heat would do fast work. We returned to the laboratory and washed up.

"Write the death certificate before the ambulance gets here," I said calmly.

He did not answer and I divined that his remorse had already begun.

Now he must register his crime in black and white, set down evidence that could send him to jail at any time. He was not afraid of the prison so much, but he had lost his last shred of self-respect.

"Sorry. I would write it myself, but I'm not the coroner. Besides, it was your duty to take care of the victims of the crash."

"I'm being blackmailed," he said with a wan smile, but I knew he meant it. He was dangerous. He might give us both away in one of his fits of pathological depression.

"Want a drink?" I asked.

He looked up, astonished, read my thoughts, and shook his head.

"You don't have to get me drunk for me to write the certificate," he muttered, walking over to the desk. "What's the man's name?"

When I told him he paled.

"W. H. Donovan," he repeated, and sat down trembling. I waited for him to recover. "We have stolen Donovan's brain!"

He laughed suddenly, turned to the desk, picked up a pen, and took a blank coroner's report from his pocket.

"I had better leave the name off," he said. "I just hope the heat melts that carcass away before every doctor in the country comes poking his nose into it."

He wrote and passed the paper to me.

"Death due to bleeding and shock preceding amputation of both legs," I read.

"They can see for themselves it's true what I wrote down." He spoke swaggeringly to hide his uneasiness and walked over to the door. "I'll see that Phoenix collects it."

He put on his big hat and walked away without glancing at me or saying good-by. He was walking out on me again.

He stopped outside for a moment to talk to Janice. They have a curious conspiracy I have never bothered to intrude on and I was not interested now in what they were saying to each other, but I went into my bedroom and called her.

Janice entered at once.

"You ought to sleep a little"; she dropped the suggestion casually. For the first time in years she was telling me what to do. She was tapping hesitantly at the door to my consciousness, timidly trying to remind me of her.

"The ambulance from Phoenix will call for the body. If anyone calls, don't disturb me whoever it is." I sank on the bed. I really needed some sleep.

Even while I was turning to the wall, I could feel sleep blacking out my mind.

SEPTEMBER 18

I WOKE at a very early morning hour. There was food near the bed, where Janice had left it in a thermos to keep warm. I ate hastily and went back to the laboratory. I heard Janice moving in her room, but she did not leave it.

Through the garden window I could see that the body had been taken away. On my desk lay the evening paper and a message. The hospital at Phoenix had phoned for me to come over and report to the coroner. Since Schratt was the coroner in the case, I tossed the paper into the wastebasket.

The Phoenix *Herald* had a big headline:

"Tycoon Dies. W. H. Donovan Killed in Plane. Crash in Snake Mountains."

I put the paper into a drawer of my desk and turned to Donovan's brain.

The pump was faithfully supplying blood to the main artery, and the ultraviolet lights shone through the glass tubes in which the serum circulated.

I wheeled the table with the encephalograph close to the vessel which contained the brain and fastened the five electrodes to the cortical tissue. One near the right ear, two high on the forehead, one above each eye cavity.

The brain of any living creature has an electric beat that is conducted by neurons, not by blood vessels or connecting tissue. All cells show varying degrees of mechanical, thermal, electrical, and chemical activity.

I switched on the current that drove the small motor, which, in turn, drew out a white paper strip an inch per second at a frequency of sixty cycles. A pen scratched a faint line on the moving paper. I amplified the infinitesimally small currents the brain was sending until their power was great enough to move the pen.

On the paper strip the activity of Donovan's thought processes showed in exact, equal curves. The curves repeated themselves; the brain was at rest, not really thinking now. The pen drew smooth alpha curves, concise as breathing.

I tested the occipital lead. The deflections were continuous, ten cycles per second, with very low seven to eight cycles per second waves.

I touched the glass and at once the alpha waves disappeared. The brain in the glass was aware that I was standing there!

Delta waves appeared on the moving strip, a sure indication that the brain was emotionally disturbed.

It seemed fatigued, however, and suddenly it fell asleep again. I saw the repeating pattern reappear. The brain slept deeply, its strength exhausted by the grave operation.

I watched its depthless slumber while the pattern of this sleep, drawn by a pen on white paper, slipped through my fingers.

I watched for hours. I knew I had succeeded.

Donovan's brain would live though his body had died.

SEPTEMBER 19

THE hospital in Phoenix phoned three times asking me to come over and answer some questions about Donovan's death.

Janice told them I was too busy now and would see them later.

Schratt called too. Janice took the phone into her room and had a long conversation with him. Generally she dislikes talking at length, so I anticipated that the situation in Phoenix was becoming involved.

When the hospital called for the fourth time, I decided to go before they became suspicious.

Janice wanted to ride into town with me. She sat silent and tense in the car. It annoyed me to feel her watching me out of the corner of her eye.

I made up my mind to clear all the accumulated issues between us as soon as possible. I resented her intensity, which interfered with my work. I had to end this household disharmony.

When we arrived in town, Janice decided to stay in the car. I did not ask why she had suddenly changed her mind or why she had bothered to ride with me at all. I went into the hospital.

At the entrance a thin shabby-looking man with a camera took pictures of me and I did not like it.

The nurse at the reception desk sent me straight up to Dr. Higgins, the superintendent.

In Higgins's waiting-room sat Schratt, dilapidated and looking greenish. I nodded at him, but his shifting eyes registered no recognition. As I was walking over to speak to him, Higgins opened a door and called me inside.

Webster, a manager of the airline, was with him. Webster did not wait for formalities. "Dr. Cory," he said, "Schratt tells me you led the emergency party to the ranger station."

"Yes," I replied. "It was the obvious thing to do. If Dr. Schratt had had to form a rescue party in Konapah, he would have arrived much later."

"As I understand it, you are not a practicing physician in this district?" Higgins spoke sharply, but I was prepared for the question.

"I am a medical doctor, Mr. Higgins." I spoke as sharply as he. "In an emergency every physician has his duty to perform."

I turned to Webster. He nodded perfunctorily as if I had ordered him to affirm my statement.

Webster was uneasy. The man who had died was too important to be disposed of with just an ordinary report. Every newspaper in the country will blow up this incident.

Webster's activities the night of the disaster will be discussed in detail.

Donovan could not have been saved if all the specialists of the Mayo clinic had been waiting at the spot of the accident, and Higgins seemed to know it. But Webster *was* to blame that an old crackpot doctor was in charge the night of the disaster and an unknown physician undertook a major operation on one of the richest men in America.

It was to my advantage that Webster urgently wished to hush up the facts and have the incident closed as quickly as possible. But Higgins, on the warpath, was out for blood. He called Schratt in.

Schratt was shaky on his feet. He looked far from presentable as the physician for an emergency airfield. Webster gazed at him with misgivings and Higgins turned away as if disgusted by Schratt's demoralized appearance.

He said hurriedly: "Please follow me!"

I walked beside Webster with Higgins in front. Ignored and left to trail behind, Schratt grew increasingly desperate.

Schratt is so unpredictable. I was afraid he might blurt out the truth in a fit of repentance. He had tried to drown his conscience in alcohol, but like most heavy drinkers he got no relief, only a still more desperate feeling of remorse.

I slowed down a little for Schratt to catch up with me. His steps were faltering, but I was afraid to touch him for fear he would imagine I meant to help him walk straight. Even such a small gesture might have provoked a display of nerves.

Higgins was leading us to the morgue. At the door Schratt, in a brave effort at self-control, pulled himself together and straightened his shoulders.

Only the one body covered with a sheet lay in the small tiled room. I knew the corpse was Donovan's, for the linen caved in at the foot of the bier where a man's legs would ordinarily have held it up.

Higgins uncovered the body and we all stared at Donovan's decaying face. I felt a chill creeping up my spine. The bandages around the head had been tampered with.

Schratt, too, observed that they were wound differently. He stepped back, but his expression did not change. He always accepts misfortune fatalistically.

"Dr. Schratt states in the death certificate that Mr. Donovan died following amputation of both legs. You did not, by any chance, bring those extremities back with you, Dr. Cory?" Higgins inquired.

"If you doubt the necessity for the operation, you had better exhume the legs. You'll find them buried at the Ranger station," I said coldly, resenting the insinuation.

Webster, who wanted least of all a further medical inquiry, quickly interrupted.

"If Donovan had died instantly, we would have been spared these fruitless post-mortems." He turned to the door. "I think there is no use discussing the case further. It won't bring Donovan back to life and may only arouse controversy."

He was putting it plainly to Higgins that he wanted the incident closed, but Higgins ignored the plea.

"The report did not mention a head injury," Higgins continued stubbornly.

"You found the ribs are broken, too," I answered quietly, knowing what he was up to. "Do you want that stated also? Are you trying to charge me with negligence? Just what is the complaint? I did all I could do."

Higgins pondered. He sensed Schratt's mounting panic, but he did not know what caused it, and that made him uncertain.

"Let's go," Webster urged. "I'm feeling a little weak. I'm not accustomed to . . ."

He opened the door of the morgue and inhaled deeply, as if trying to keep from fainting.

We left. I felt cold sweat on my forehead and did not raise my head for fear of betraying myself. We went back to Higgins's office.

"You'd better change physicians, Mr. Webster." Higgins had to slaughter some scapegoat. "Dr. Schratt has clearly neglected his duty. It was up to him to go at once to the scene of the disaster, not to send anyone else. But, as I understand it, Dr. Schratt was incapacitated."

Schratt lifted his flabby, bloated face. He looked crushed.

"I'm obliged to dismiss you," Webster said to him hurriedly, glad to have found a way to satisfy Higgins. "Sorry, Dr. Schratt."

Webster looked at me inquisitively and added: "Since I

must have a physician in residence near the emergency field, perhaps Dr. Cory could take over these duties."

He looked at Higgins for approval, but I was in a mood to put both men in their places.

"I'm not interested," I said gruffly, and walked to the door.

Higgins followed me. His attitude changed at once when he saw I could not be bullied.

"Dr. Cory." His tone was conciliatory. "I'm sorry. You see I had to investigate. . . ."

I looked at him coldly.

"Donovan's family are here. At the De Anza. Please do me a favor. Go and see them. They are anxious to talk to you."

"All right," I answered, grabbing my hat, and left without a good-by.

I still felt uneasy. Higgins had acted strangely. Did he know I had removed Donovan's brain?

Who had looked beneath Donovan's bandages?

I heard steps behind me. It was Schratt, who passed without looking up as if I were responsible for his misfortune.

I left the hospital and walked straight across the market place to the De Anza Hotel. I passed my car and Janice was not in it.

When I asked for Mr. Donovan, the room clerk treated me as if I were a millionaire too.

A bellboy took me all the way up to the fourth floor. He confided in an awed voice that the management had closed all the rooms on that floor except the suite occupied by Howard Donovan and his sister, Chloe Barton.

The way he spoke Chloe Barton's name told me she was good-looking.

It was her brother who received me, a man of forty-five, heavily built and tall, with the same skull conformation as his father's. He stood back of the writing-desk, rustled through papers a moment as if he were looking for something, then suddenly, straight into my face, he said:

"I'm glad you came, Dr. Cory."

Howard Donovan continued to scrutinize me embarrassingly, as if I were there for a cross-examination and he were the prosecuting attorney. His money had given him an exaggerated conception of his own importance and a fine contempt for other people. He ignored my resentment.

On his desk lay his father's worn, blood-stained wallet, an old-fashioned watch, and the small notebook that had been found on Donovan senior.

Howard Donovan spoke almost without moving his lips, as if he were miserly even with words.

"I wanted to thank you, Dr. Cory," he said slowly as if the words had been torn from his mouth. "I'm sure you did everything for my father that could be done."

I was tempted not to answer in the affirmative, just to study his reaction. When I said nothing, he moved his bulk nimbly across the thick carpet toward a door.

"I want you to meet my sister," he muttered. He stopped at the door, turned toward me with his hand on the knob, then knocked rather softly and called his sister's name.

Chloe Barton entered. She was a dark-haired girl with white teeth and straight shoulders, very conscious of her looks. She greeted me and sat down, folding her hands in her lap in a graceful, unnatural pose.

I knew women like this well from my years at the hospital. They have to have the admiration of a male before they can be at ease with themselves. They are erotomaniacs, only happy as long as they are sure of a man's adoration.

Her nose, short and turned up showed a slight thickening of the lesser alar cartilage, a sure sign that it had been worked on by a plastic surgeon.

I remembered her story. She had been a stout, plain girl with a hooked nose, had married three times in quick succession and always big brutal men. After the third unhappy marriage, which ended in a scandal, she had her nose remodeled and changed her character completely.

She dieted away forty pounds and when she found she had become handsome, she enwrapped herself in a new aura as in a cloak, became elusive with her friends, egocentric to the point of mental unbalance. She gave up her promiscuousness and concentrated on herself in a quiet, narcissistic way.

"We wanted to thank you for making my poor father's death easier."

Chloe Barton spoke as if she had studied the sentence. Not a muscle in her face twitched. The transparent skin remained pale. "We want to know what he said before he died—what message he left for his children."

Howard Donovan had stepped behind the desk again and was watching me intently. The light from the window fell hard on my face, while he was in semi-darkness. Chole's lips were curved in a frozen smile. I could not make out what they expected to hear, but it seemed of great importance to them.

"I must disappoint you," I said. "I don't remember."

Mrs. Barton seemed shocked by my words and turned to Howard Donovan with undissimulated consternation.

"I wish he could remember," the girl said, as if it was up to Howard to make me do it.

Howard nodded, and said to me: "It's extremely important to us. Just try to remember a few words."

They stared at me again as if to read some secret they thought I was hiding. I could only shrug my shoulders.

"Listen, Dr. Cory," Howard Donovan insisted, "we'll make it worth your while." He seemed to think I was purposely holding something back. With a quick gesture, he snatched up the blood-stained wallet as if to give it to me.

"I can't tell you anything." I was annoyed. "Your father was unconscious all the time. Anything he did say didn't make sense."

"Are you sure?" Howard asked sharply.

The scene was embarrassing.

"Quite sure!" I took my hat. "Following extreme loss of blood no one can talk coherently."

I walked toward the door, but Chloe called after me:

"We want to pay you for trying to save my father's life."

"No charge," I answered, and walked out.

Their behavior was very mysterious. Obviously they were afraid the old man had confided in me. I thought of Donovan but could not recall anything he had said.

I went to my car and drove off. I wanted to get out of this town, fast. Watching so many faces, listening to so many voices, being cross-charged with so many mental currents upset me.

My work demanded concentration. I was groping in the

dark tunnel of science, developing my sense of touch. These annoying disturbances were blinding lights in the darkness that stunned and left me bewildered.

I had to get hold of myself, calm down, arrest the wildly swinging membrane of my powers of concentration.

Higgins, Webster, Schratt—I wanted to banish them all from my mind, but they kept creeping back.

When I had driven a few miles, I realized I had forgotten Janice. She should have stayed in the car!

Moving along the straight highway and concentrating on the point of the end where the macadam seemed to lance the horizon, I suddenly knew how to watch the brain more closely.

At rest, relaxing, it was sending out ten-cycle alpha waves. As soon as it reacted to a stimulus, the alpha frequencies changed to beta, with twenty fluctuations per second. If I sent the amplified alpha wave through an alternate circuit which in turn was connected with an electric bulb, any change of frequency would change the circuit and switch on the lamp.

When the brain was thinking the bulb would burn. When the bulb was dark the brain would be at rest. How simple!

I drove home as fast as I could, jumped out of the car, and rushed to the door of the laboratory, but entered quietly, not to disturb the brain.

It was asleep, the encephalograph showed.

Silently I went to work, connected the amplifier with the relay and connected an electric bulb on the circuit.

I switched on the current and watched the lamp.

Producing alpha frequencies, the brain was at rest.

I tapped at the vessel in which the organ was suspended and at once it became aware of the disturbance. The encephalograph registered delta waves, the alpha cycles were blocked out, the relay cut in on the current and lighted the bulb!

I stared at the miracle and sat down to rejoice.

The lamp went out again; the brain was relaxing. But when I got up, it felt my movement and the light reappeared.

Crossing to my desk to register the time of my discovery, I had another idea. If the brain had emotions and perceptions, it was thinking systematically. It was aware of out-side disturbances certainly, or its alpha waves would not have changed to beta or delta frequencies. Without a doubt a precise thought process was going on in this eyeless, earless matter.

It might, like a blind man, feel the light or, like a deaf one, perceive sound. It might, in its dark mute existence, produce thoughts of immense clarity and inspiration. It might, just because it was cut off from the distractions of the senses, be able to concentrate all its brain-power on important thoughts.

I wanted to know those thoughts! But how could I get in touch with the brain?

It could not talk or move, yet if I could study its thinking, I might learn about the great unsolved riddles of nature. The brain might, in its complete solitude, have created answers to eternal questions.

I heard a car stop. It was Schratt bringing Janice home. I was disturbed, of course. The noise of the auto, Janice's footsteps, the pronounced quiet opening of the front door, shoved my thoughts off their narrow track.

I waited till Janice had gone to her room, but I could not concentrate again. I left the laboratory and knocked at her door.

She called me and I entered.

Janice was sitting on the bed, her face turned toward me, her hands on her knees, her body hunched over as if she were weighed down in thought.

"Sorry I had to leave Phoenix without you," I said to begin this conversation which must clear the issues between us once and for all.

"Schratt brought me home," she answered soberly.

"May I sit down?" I asked. I had not been in her room for months.

She nodded and went on in the same quiet voice. "Schratt lost his job." She looked at me as if I could have prevented his misfortune.

"I know. What could I do?" I replied.

She nodded again, but not in confirmation of my words. "You did nothing to help him."

For a moment I was stunned. Was this a rebuke from Janice?

"Did he say so?"

"He's desperate," she answered.

"Like most drunkards, he shows signs of Korsakow's psychosis, if you remember the symptoms from your lectures. Lessening of the power of observation, inability to correlate new experiences with the apperceptive mass, conjectures, retrograde amnesia, altogether polyneuritis alcoholic!"

Her face was sad.

"I've invited him to live with us," she said. "I hope you won't refuse. He can have the room off the back garden and he won't disturb you."

Her kindness had no limits. She would have filled the house with hoboes if I were willing.

"Now we're stuck with him for the rest of his life! Pretty smart! I have to buy his discretion. He knows that he knows too much and he means to cash in on it."

She did not answer, but she paled and her mouth grew very white.

It was her house. She could do whatever she liked with it. She paid for all the machines and experiments. I was completely dependent on her and she never said a word about it. She may even never have thought of it.

But I wanted to be free!

Janice did not want to fight. Her expression grew soft as she withdrew into a shell where no rough word and no hard blow could reach her. She surrendered her personality and won, as she always did, by refusing to defend herself.

"All right," I said. "Did Schratt tell you Webster offered me his job? Maybe I ought to have taken it. Maybe I will."

She smiled kindly, understandingly. She knew my work consumed all my time and thought. Even the fact of our marriage had been dissolved in my work's acid domination. She knew I could not divert my strength.

Exhausted, I sat there in front of her. I knew I could not order her to leave me. Even my command would carry no conviction. And she would rather die, desiccated by hot winds and sweltering desert heat, than leave me!

She had made up her mind to stay and no unkindness,

no disregard could ever part her from me. I would have had to kill her to get rid of her.

Even this would be of no avail. Her memory would haunt me to the end of my days. My life was her life too. She would never give up. She knew I knew that, and the futility of my attacks on her gave her inexhaustible strength.

"All right, let Schratt stay here."

I gave up wearily. I had solved nothing. She had only bound herself to me more securely.

SEPTEMBER 25

I HAVE moved my bed into the laboratory. I want to live as close as possible to the object of my experiment.

I eat alone, never leave the laboratory, never see Janice and Schratt. From time to time I hear Schratt's car arrive or leave. Franklin brings my food but, well trained, he never distracts me by talking.

I ordered him to collect news about Donovan's death and he transmitted my wish to Janice. Now nearly every day he brings in newspapers or magazines with stories about Donovan. I have read them all and soon I knew as much about Donovan's life as if we had been intimates.

Between myself and the brain in the respirator a very close relationship has developed. It is not just dumb, mute matter, kept alive by a pump, going on existing aimlessly. It is a living organ, ductile in its reactions and responsive to stimuli like a human being.

After public curiosity at the first briefly reported news of the crash and its victim was exhausted, gossip began to reveal sordid details of Donovan's private life.

The more I read about him, the more his character darkens. He, like all the great money-makers, was unscrupulous to a criminal degree. Only a limited amount of money can be honestly earned. To amass millions in the short course of a life one must be ruthless and untroubled by a conscience.

Nobody knows for certain how much money Donovan

made, but he owned the biggest mail-order house in the world. It sprawled like an octopus over all the states.

Donovan was sixty-five when the plane cracked up, no age for a strong man to die. He was traveling with his lawyer and two pilots. A few days before his death he had turned over the reins of the business to his son. It was a surprise to all of them—his board of directors and especially his family.

Why Donovan, a man whose only incentive all his life had been a craving for more and more power, suddenly sloughed off his authority, the papers could not reveal. He had undertaken the plane trip to his Miami house without informing his family or friends. There has been specualtion about quarrels with his son and daughter. A paper hinted at a disease, but nobody knows for sure.

I have become deeply curious about Donovan's life story. The laws of human emotions are unknown, but here I have an opportunity to penetrate the mysteries of a brain, perhaps discover the factors which determine its capabilities.

Which chemical reaction creates success? Which one is responsible for our failures? Which produces happiness—which misery?

Donovan's brain may supply the answers.

For hours I let the encephalogram run through my fingers and tried to find a relation between the form of the pen-curves and the thoughts they must express.

We know that when the brain imagines a tree these curves are different from those when it thinks of a horse or an automobile. An emotional outburst of hatred draws different lines from those of pleasure.

It is within possibility to find a code which translates the relation between the reading of the encephalograph and the mental image. If I could find the key, the brain could communicate with me.

I cannot talk to it for it has no organ of hearing. It cannot see or taste. But without doubt it is sensitive to touch. When I knock at the glass vessel the brain receives the sound-waves and reacts.

If it thinks, a process I cannot determine, only assume, I should be able to tap messages to it.

The problem is how to receive an answer.

FOR days I have tried to transmit the same phrase to the brain in Morse:—— . . . . . —— . — . — —— . . . . —— . . . . . . — . —— — . !

Listen, Donovan! Listen, Donovan!

The encephalograph has reacted, but always differently, in beta and delta frequencies. Never the same pattern twice.

It occurred to me the brain might not understand the code. Donovan probably knew nothing about telegraphy. A simple explanation for my failure!

Though the brain can conceive only what it has experienced, however, it might be possible to add to the sum of its knowledge by training.

Patiently I began to tap out the Morse signals against the glass vessel: . — A, — . . . B.

I went on indefatigably for days and nights, whenever I found the bulb at the relay burning to indicate the brain was awake. I was sometimes disheartened, for no sign indicated the brain understood what I wanted.

But the brain seemed to be watching me. The beta curves were smooth and precise, as if it concentrated on what I was doing. When I stopped tapping, the frequencies on the paper tape changed.

Donovan's brain might be trying to send a message to me.

OCTOBER 2

I REPEATED the Morse signs thousands of times, perfunctorily, sometimes half asleep. In my dreams I became an instrument myself, repeating the signs unendingly. As I tapped out the letters of the alphabet over and over again, they would have sunk into the memory of a baby. A brain as intelligent and versatile as Donovan's *must* realize there was a pattern in this, must remember it, even automatically, must decipher the meaning.

Again I began: Listen, Donovan! Can you understand? Donovan! If you understand, think three times of a tree, Donovan. Three times "Tree." Tree! Tree! Tree!

I watched the encephalogram. The pen moved convulsively and formed a sign, the same sign, three times. The wild delta waves shook the pen as if in confusion.

Exhausted, I slumped on my bed, unable to organize my thoughts. Was I mistaken? Had the brain really answered me? The encephalogram had showed the same curve three times, but did that prove that Donovan had understood?

Theoretical concepts outside the experimental proof are meaningless. I had to dismiss specuoltion. I can accept only the proof my instruments supply.

Again I tried: Think of a tree, three times. Tree, tree, tree.

The sign appeared, once, twice, again! The same sign!

Then alpha cycles flowed into beta frequencies, smooth, repeating. The brain, exhausted, had fallen asleep.

I could measure its deep slumber. The deflections became wider. The brain was dreaming. The pen on the paper strip moved wildly. The brain was having a nightmare!

OCTOBER 3

THE same night, last night, I went out to Schratt's room behind the garage. I was at my wits' end and had to talk to him.

The brain had obeyed my command and repeated the words I told it to think. But how could I translate its own thoughts, which no doubt were written in the scrawls on the paper strip. I am impatient, afraid the brain may die in the midst of my observations. My time is limited.

It was three o'clock in the morning. The sky was clear. Freezing cold made the sand crackle under my feet.

Without knocking I stepped into Schratt's room. He was deep in sleep, his mouth open. His face was thinner, but he looked healthy. The bloated skin had tightened and some color had come into his coarse cheeks. Janice's saintly influence has deprived him of his liquor, I assume.

He suddenly opened his eyes and stared at me as if he thought me a ghost. When I spoke his name, he sat up but still stared.

"Come with me," I said. My voice sounded hoarse.

I must have frightened Schratt for I saw fear and suspicion in his eyes. I was looking into a bottomless pit: he was afraid I might cut him up to stick him into my test tubes. He thought me capable of anything to further my researches.

"I want to show you something," I said.

The frightened look did not leave his eyes, but he crawled out of bed and pulled on a dirty old bathrobe. He seemed to be thinking seriously, his forehead furrowed. Finally he sat down again and spoke with desperate determination.

"I'm not interested in your experiments, Patrick."

He had made up his mind to have no part in my work. He was more detached from me now, living in my house, than he had been in the days when he stormed out of the laboratory resolving never to see me again.

"You must help me, Schratt. I can't continue without you."

That was the most flattering appeal I could think of. He was visibly moved, but drawing the robe closer about his fat body, he still stubbornly shook his head.

For him, and for me too, the whole world was a laboratory. But I used it and he shied away from new knowledge. He had withdrawn into a monkish seclusion, abjuring himself as a scientist.

"You know I detest your researches, Patrick. They can't help humanity! All they could do is promote unhappiness. They take the world back to barbarism."

"I'm a specialist and you too," I replied, to help him argue himself out of these notions. "Civilization cannot exist without specilization."

"I'm not interested in civilization. We are so ignorant of our souls we take refuge in mechanics, physics, chemistry. We are losing our consciousness of the human dignity that distinguished man from animal. You are making the human being a highly specialized stone-age man ruled by egotism. You are creating a mechanical, synthetic life and killing the spirit that has lifted humanity above the beast. You believe only your test tubes. You are killing faith! I'm glad only a few men like you exist! Your researches have made you more and more rational, until you refuse to recognize a single fact cannot be proved in the laboratory. I'm frightened, Patrick! You're creating a mechanical soul that will destroy the world."

I listened patiently. Schratt obviously had thought deeply about all this, and saying it seemed to make him feel better.

"Great mathematicians and physiologists," I said quietly, "inevitably arrive at a point where their minds meet something beyond human comprehension, something divine. They can only face it by believing in God. Most scientists become religious when they reach that stage of research."

Schratt looked at me astonished. Those might have been his own words. When he saw I had not spoken with irony, he nodded, but doubtfully, still mistrusting me as a convert to his philosophy.

"However," I began again at once when I saw his suspicion that I had deceived him, "However, to come to this point of submission to the great holy unknown, man first must travel through the sphere he is capable of exploring. Somewhere where our intelligence has its limits the road of our research ends. We juggle the incomprehensible to arrive at the concrete. We use a symbol for the infinite, dividing concrete figures with it, adding a plus, a minus to it, as if we could visualize the shape of the boundless. We use the infinite to count with, as if it were tangible. But nobody comprehends its nature. We penetrate regions beyond our intelligence and return with solutions to our problems. Whom do we hurt? Not even ourselves! I cannot give up my research because fear prompts me not to go on. At the end of the road I am traveling stands God, who speaks not in formulas but in monosyllables. I want to stand close enough to Him to hear His yes or no!"

Schratt looked through me with a far-away expression.

"Salvation must be earned by deeds, not by negation," I concluded.

I walked to the door and waited.

37

The moon shone clear as a white sun in the transparent sky and myriads of stars filmed the firmament.

I had not looked at the sky in years.

I heard Schratt murmur, and after a minute he came out of his room.

He followed me into the laboratory, still doubtful and defensive. "What is it you want me to see?"

"The brain is communicating with me," I said. I pointed out how the relay was connected. The brain was asleep, the lamp dark.

I knocked at the glass vessel and the lamp began to glow.

Schratt stood staring at the bulb, unwilling to reveal his desire to hear how I had accomplished this step.

I told him how I had communicated with the brain and taught it Morse. Schratt listened motionless, like a man confronted by something supernatural.

I knocked at the vessel and told it to think of a tree, three times.

The encephalogram showed unmistakably congruent curves, repeated them three times.

Schratt slumped onto my bed and nodded. He forgot his determination not to interest himself in the experiment. He stared awed at the vessel, the instruments, the encephalograph. Schratt *is* a genius. He never doubted the evidence of his eyes. Only an extraordinary mind can accept a new thing at once. He did. He understood it.

I sat down too. I gave him time to overcome his excitement. Finally he got up, stepped over to the vessel, and gingerly ran a thick forefinger along the electric connection to the encephalograph. When the bulb suddenly glowed, he nodded and murmured. His coarse bloated face shone with an inner light.

"The brain is alive," he said as if he had discovered a cosmic truth. "No doubt it is alive! We must find a way to get its messages."

He sat down heavily again and half closed his eyes, thinking. He did not seem discouraged by the apparent hopelessness of the task he was setting himself.

He ran the paper strip through his fingers and examined it closely.

"Alpha, beta, and delta frequencies," he said. "But they can't be deciphered."

He dropped the strip, discarding the idea of reading its curves.

"There's no possibility of decoding that," he said definitely. "You tried, didn't you?"

I nodded.

"You went at it the wrong way. And you knew it. . . ."

I began to defend my theory to make him prove I was wrong.

"If you registered every thought-wave on a paper strip," I said, "and made yourself familiar with its curve, you ought to be able to compare the encephalogram from Donovan's brain with your own thought dictionary. Assume I register my encephalogram of the word *horse*. Wouldn't Donovan, thinking the same word, produce the same curve? Comparing it with mine, couldn't I determine its meaning? Why could we not similarly decode messages from Donovan's brain? Sound waves and brain waves are similar in design. Brain waves move between ½ and 60 cycles per second, sound waves between 10 and 16,000. Sound has wider variation than thought."

I knew I was wrong but I wanted to hear him refute the theory.

Schratt shook his head. "A sound wave has fixed frequency, but thought-waves differ with each individual. My brain does not produce the same waves as yours, and even the daily changing state of your health influences the microvolt output of your cells. The flux of every idea is dependent on the microvoltage the brain produces, and that varies from minute to minute. It changes when you excite yourself, when you feel sick, when you are well. No! We must discard the theory of reading the encephalogram like a telegraph message."

He was right. But what other approach is there?

"We could try to get in touch with it by telepathy," he pondered.

I was astonished at him. I would never have considered such an unorthodox method, approaching an unknown medium by using an unknown component.

I must have shaken my head in disapproval, for he continued: "Why not? Let's use this idea as an *a priori* and not wait for the slow gathering of experimental evidence! The brain produces micro short waves. The surrounding air is permanently electrically charged with 9,000 frequencies. Our brain waves send out oscillations that disturb the electric field of the atmosphere, which in turn conducts the waves to the receiver. The thinking brain is the transmitter, the other brain the receiver."

"What other brain?" I asked.

"Yours," he said.

He stared at me, snorted and nodded, furrowed his brow and nodded again, as if he had already proved his theory.

"You have just handed me a theoretical analysis of the phenomenon of telepathy," I said dryly, "and it's primitive."

"There is clarity in simplification," he answered earnestly, without conceit.

Conceit sets a limit to wisdom and Schratt lacks conceit to the point of self-negation.

I pondered the explanation.

Brain number one the transmitter, brain number two the receiver, the surrounding air the electric field.

All this could be proved. The encephalograph verified the fact that the brain released microvolts. The electric field of the surrounding air can be measured. But what about the receiving end, the second brain? How could we know that it would transform micro-waves back into thoughts which had originated in another brain?

There was, simply, a body of public testimony and my own personal experience that telepathy is not a fake.

A thought created in the mind of person number one *can* be received by person number two. It is plausible that our brain works like a radio station.

"Granting your theory of the working of telepathy is true, how could we apply it to this problem?" I asked.

"Try," Schratt said, gropingly. "Try to cut out your own thoughts. Donovan's thoughts might transmit themselves to you."

"I might imagine things. I want a fool-proof test," I said, impatient.

"There are plenty of famous mediums," he suggested.

"We might get a faker," I answered. I had expected

something better from Schratt than this unhealthy suggestion. "We're in a laboratory, not at a spiritualist séance."

Schratt paced up and down, murmuring to himself, shaking his head. He was pursuing the truth and I, instead of helping, had rejected his groping suggestions.

"Give me time," he said. "We will find it."

He walked to the door and left without a good-by.

The morning had come up. Dawn lighted the sky.

I felt tired. My thoughts were not coherent. This state of weakness, I recognized, might increase my receptiveness. Schratt's theory might work!

I pushed a chair close to the brain. It was awake. The lamp was burning.

I stared at the grayish mass of nerve tissue whose energies were changing thoughts into electric currents. I tried to clear the path for the message Donovan might have for me.

OCTOBER 6

AFTER experimenting unsuccessfully for days I have discarded telepathy.

Donovan's brain is unadapted to it. The central nervous system consists of cerebrum, cerebellum, and spinal cord. But Donovan's brain lacks the co-operation of the spinal cord, and by itself it cannot produce enough power to influence my nervous system.

I find myself at the dreaded borderline where experiments reach a dead end. A new approach to the problem is needed, but I have no new ideas. Wherever I look I face a blank wall.

Schratt has not discussed the problem with me again. Since he has no further suggestions to offer, he shuns me. I have nothing to tell him either and we avoid each other.

Schratt's incapability has produced a strong remorse and I am angry at his negative attitude toward my work.

Janice fainted last night. Schratt is taking care of her. I am sure the desert heat has made her anemic. She should get away from here before she pays for her stubbornness. She has been warned often enough. I am not to blame.

Franklin brought magazines and newspapers with new stories about Donovan.

One showed his funeral at Forest Lawn. Behind the coffin walked his son Howard and Chloe, his daughter.

Now Donovan is cremated and the last clue is destroyed. I am safe.

Donovan never thought his days would end so soon. He left no will.

A man does not leave power to withdraw aimlessly from his duties. A man wants to retire either to enjoy living or because he is to die soon. Donovan did not give up the reins of a hundred-million-dollar corporation to play golf in Florida or read books. He was a man to whom work was life itself and he could not have lived on when his activities stopped. He knew that, but he resigned from everything that he had lived for. There is some secret behind it.

The papers have speculated and rumored that Donovan had hid millions away. During the last years of his life he withdrew great sums of cash that have not been found in his private bank accounts.

A story in one of the Sunday magazine sections was called "The Mansion of Lost Millions." It showed Donovan's Florida house, a big sprawling building where the money is supposed to be hidden. Here was a crude drawing of Howard attacking the wood paneling with an axe while Chloe, drawn with all emphasis on her sex, looked on with burning eyes.

One paper had my picture as I entered the hospital in Phoenix and my house here in Washington Junction. A photo, too, of Janice and my car. I remember the shabby-looking photographer, who came here for information.

"Dr. Patrick Cory, mysterious physician who operated on W. H. Donovan and in whose arms the millionaire died," read the caption.

There was a drawing of me in White's kitchen, dramatically holding the dying man, which said: "Did the millionaire whisper his secrets into the doctor's ear?"

White was depicted at the station, pointing to the grave where Donovan's legs are buried. And in a drawing of the plane wreckage, arrows marked the spots where the bodies were found. The press has missed few tricks. Then I threw the papers away. I was not interested in Donovan's life. My concern was the brain's future.

I had a telephone call about making a report on the accident to the airline commission in Phoenix. Since I want to have the inquiries behind me, I sent in my report speedily.

I want them to forget Donovan.

OCTOBER 7

LAST night I had an impulse to turn on the radio in the living-room. I do not know what impelled me: I never listen to it. Actually I dislike this instrument, which only distracts me, but impulse born in the subconscious sometimes motivates action which seems without purpose. I recognize this extra-sensory faculty and never resist.

Janice was still up, mending one of Schratt's shirts. I was struck again by her anemic look. She has lost weight considerably. When I entered she put her work down, thinking I wanted to talk to her, but I turned on the radio.

I found a short-wave Spanish broadcast, turned the dial, and a French one came in, less clear, the fadings sometimes blotting out the music. I dialed again and an American coast-to-coast hook-up came through strongly. Suddenly I knew what I was looking for and the inspiration made me flush hotly.

I rushed out to Schratt's room to tell him what I had discovered.

He sat up, then jumped out of bed with fright, grabbing his greasy bathrobe. "Has anything happened to Janice?"

"She is all right," I said.

The fear floated out of Schratt's face, but there was still despair.

"She's in bad shape, you know," he said.

My impatience left no time to discuss Janice.

"I've told her to go back to New England. Perhaps you can make her do it!"

Schratt looked at me and I did not like the look. It was not for him to criticize me, but I needed him.

"I think I'm on the right track," I said soberly, not wanting to become drunk with my own enthusiasm and arrive at a wrong conclusion.

Schratt did not speak. I had a feeling he resented my indifference toward Janice.

"I tried our your suggestion of telepathy, but Donovan's brain is not strong enough," I said. "Thoughts cannot be amplified by electrical devices. But there is a way of making them stronger."

I saw he was interested, and it made me feel I was on the right track. I continued:

"To give you an example: If you broadcast from a station with a weak transmitter, a receiver cannot amplify the sound waves beyond a certain distance, and increasing the power of the receiver does not help. The power of the transmitter has to be increased."

I waited for Schratt to digest my thoughts, but he still did not see what I was driving at. I went on.

"We must increase the electric thought discharge of Donovan's brain until it can contact a sensitive brain."

Schratt grasped the idea, but he could not perceive at once the method I was contemplating.

"If the vesicular or gray cells," I explained, "could be charged with ten thousand or more microvolts instead of with ten to one hundred, the output of the telepathic power would increase tenfold. It might become strong enough for the brain to influence every living being."

Schratt nodded, but fearfully. "You may be right, Patrick," he said slowly, "but—"

He hesitated. I hated his reluctance, his negative attitude. I wanted help, not discouragement.

"Don't start throwing ethical monkey wrenches into the works again!" I said hotly. "I must go forward. I have no time for ideals outside my researches."

"You're dealing with a power you might not be able to control," Schratt said monkishly. "Brain-power is unlimited, and unpredictable. . . ."

"Should experiments stop because they might become dangerous?" I asked, tired of him and his cowardice. "I can terminate my research anytime I please."

"How?"

"Shut off the pump. Cut off the circulating blood and Donovan's brain will die."

"Let me think it over," he answered, but I left his room.

OCTOBER 10

INSTALLED another ultraviolet lamp, added fresh blood serum to the arterial blood to carry away the CO_2 more quickly. Prepared a new blood plasma, enriched it with concentrated bases, acids, salts, animoacids, fats, proteins, so that it had the proper hydrogen in concentration.

I want to overfeed the brain. The increase in nourishing substance will affect the metabolism, increase the sum of the chemical and tissue changes.

OCTOBER 12

THE encephalograms are more vivid, alpha frequencies have disappeared completely. The brain does not relax any more, but it falls asleep more frequently.

The lamp burned only six hours and thirty-eight minutes yesterday, six hours and twenty-five minutes today. The increased nourishment seems to have a soporific effect and the brain sleeps as if recuperating. The demand for sleep increases in direct proportion to the brain's gain in strength.

OCTOBER 14

ELECTRICAL potential and electric capacity have increased to five hundred and ten microvolts.

New tissue cells have added to the gray matter. Since every normal lobe of the human brain has been identified, named, and examined, I wonder what functions these new enlargements can have.

SCHRATT came to see me. I showed him the enlarged brain and demonstrated its reactions. The electric beat has increased to more than a thousand microvolts. Soon I shall be able to measure with an ordinary voltmeter.

Schratt has been thinking about how to feed the brain. He has brought back human brain ash from the Phoenix morgue. It contains all the elements of which the living organ is comprised. It is far more efficent to add tissue ash to the blood serum than to mix in dozens of gland extracts.

I should have thought of that myself.

I thanked Schratt and he used the opportunity to talk about Janice. She is leaving for Los Angles, and he asked me to see her.

He spoke seriously as if he has only been thinking of my problem in exchange for something he wanted me to do.

I promised to see Janice before she leaves.

THROUGH a criminal negligence I produced an electric short. I dropped a pair of pliers and the 110-volt line for the pump short-circuited.

There was a spark at the edge of the vessel, the pump stopped, and the encephalogram was blotted out. The pen ran straight.

I repaired the wiring as fast as I could and the pump started again, but the brain did not react.

I was petrified with fear lest I had killed it!

I added half a cc. of 1-1000 adrenalin to the serum.

After a few minutes the lamp began to glow and the pen moved in excited delta waves.

I was exhausted and faint.

The electric equipment must be strengthened, a second pump must be installed for an emergency. At once!

I FOUND a message on the pad I use for notes! It was an illegible scribble written in ink.

The door of my laboratory was locked and bolted. The fingers of my left hand were ink-stained.

I seem to have got up in my sleep, taken the pen, and written these meaningless scrawls. But I never walked in my sleep before! And I do not write with my left hand!

I studied the scrawls without being able to make out a meaning. I turned the paper around until I finally recognized a definite D, a V, an A, an N, and two single letters in front, one of them unmistakably an H, the other an M or a W. The whole word was enclosed with a wavering line.

W. H. Donovan.

It was, without doubt, Donovan's name. I had written Donovan's signature with my left hand, during my sleep!

I walked over to the encephalograph, which I had left running all night. The brain was asleep, but part of the paper strip was marked with straight pen-strokes which paralleled the edge of the paper and could only have been produced in extreme excitement.

I suddenly felt weak and sat down.

I remembered that Donovan was left-handed. I had read it in one of the magazines.

Exhausted from overwork, I must have walked in my sleep and unconsciously imitated Donovan's signature. My fever to get in touch with his brain had produced this phenomenon. Considering my concentration on the experiment, it was not strange it had happened.

But suppose Donovan had ordered me to do this? During the night mental resistance is at a low ebb. This is the time to influence a mind when consciousness, latent between

47

dream and reality, can sometimes be commanded to motor responses, like walking or writing.

No! I cannot believe it!

But then the electric short may have shocked the brain into activity as the brain of a mental patient is electrically shocked into action.

OCTOBER 19

I DID NOT sleep all night, probably because I tried too hard.

I had left paper and ink handy on the desk, but I received no telepathic commands. When, sometimes, I felt and urge to get up and take the pen, I fought the impulse down, fearing it might have resulted from my nervous state and not from Donovan's influence.

I had to be sure!

The more I have thought about the scrawls on the paper, the more I am convinced that I was merely sleepwalking.

I have relapsed into deep despair, convinced my experiment is a failure.

OCTOBER 20

JANICE left today for Los Angeles.

I talked to her before Schratt took her to the station, but I do not remember the conversation.

My mind revolves around the problem of Donovan's brain. I am impatient to sleep and give Donovan a chance to get in touch with me.

Tonight I will take a sleeping draught. This may blot out my resistance.

OCTOBER 21

How stupid to have taken Veronal! It paralyzed my mind and prevented any response.

I am in such a nervous state I hear voices talking. I

must control myself. A nervous doctor is not a scientist. The best thing is not to force the experiment. To wait.

OCTOBER 25

NOTHING has happened these last days. The brain's electric output has risen to fiteen hundred microvolts and still increases.

I have lost weight. Franklin prepares the food. I realize now that Janice, knowing how little I eat, added vitamin concentrates to my food. She kept me healthy with a reinforced diet which I seem to miss now. My sudden despair and weariness are due to lack of vitamin B_1.

I am exhausted.

OCTOBER 27

I HAVE received the message. I wrote it myself, but clearly Donovan ordered me to write while I was asleep.

It is Donovan's name written shakily like a weak signature of a sick man, or it is shaky because I wrote with my left hand, as Donovan did. It is exactly Donovan's signature. I found a reproduction of it in a magazine. This is the same scrawl. The whole name enclosed in a typical oval, the same hard lines of the H, the familiar flourish of the N at the end of the word. It is not my writing at all.

The brain has found a way to get in touch with me. Probably the electric current shocked it into activity, perhaps charged the protoplasmic cells to the point of mental combustion.

I sat on the corner of my bed for hours without moving, too exhausted to think.

I want proof, more proof!

THE proof came today.

I had not administered a shock to the brain again, for the electric voltage has risen to two thousand five hundred microvolts, and I do not know how much ohm resistance the brain has.

I was sitting at my desk when I suddenly felt tired. It was a strange, soft fatigue that entered not my body, but my brain. I was still thinking, but in a hazy, drowsy fashion. Then I saw my lift hand move, take the pen, and write.

The name was written out stronger this time: Warren Horace Donovan. The long flourish encircled it again, as if to prove its authenticity.

My hand put the pen back and my own thoughts slowly returned from the back of my mind. They reappeared as if emerging from water, wavering first, then shaping up clearly.

I walked over to the vessel. Donovan's brain was awake.

"Did you ask me to write your name?" I patted out against the glass in Morse.

I waited. I repeated the message again, slower. A third time.

I walked back to the desk.

Suddenly I felt the same sensation again as my mind retreated into dimness. I was completely aware what I was doing, only the motor impulses were out of my control.

I saw my left hand pick up the pen, and in firm letters I wrote: "Warren Horace Donovan"!

THE human brain cannot work on continuously, without restoring itself at regular intervals to transform potential into electric energy again. The more intense the activity, the more sleep is needed. Donovan's brain lapses into sleep more than half the time.

Around its bare tissues a new layer of grayish-white matter is forming. Donovan's brain is growing into a new shape. A new species of creature is building here, which never before existed in this mortal world. A ball of flesh whose life depends on an electric pump and artificial feeding, but capable nevertheless of sending out energies of thought surpassing our limited strength. Every day it grows in potentiality.

It can impose its power over my thoughts whenever it pleases.

First I have the strange sensation of another will compelling the movements of my hands and feet, commanding all the motor responses of my body.

Then other thoughts than mine enter my mind. The brain, bodyless itself, uses my body with my consent to achieve an independence of its own though stolid, mute, and deaf.

I live a double existence. My thoughts retreat into the back of my mind as I observe, detached, the phenomena which Donovan's brain directs. I am then a schizophrenic, a person whose personality is split. Unlike a man suffering from intrapsychic ataxia, however, I am at all times conscious of my actions.

When Donovan's brain is asleep I am undistracted. I use this precious time to continue this report of the case.

Donovan's thinking is still incoherent. Occasionally I seem to receive a logical reply to the questions I communicate in Morse through the glass vessel. Do the vibrations thus created transmit the message to the brain? It acts like a man in fever or in sleep. It always orders me to write down the same names, which seemingly have no connection with each other.

Roger Hinds is one of the names. Anton Sternli another. Donovan's son, Howard, too, is named, but no memory of his daughter seems to enter his mind. Katherine appears quite frequently. She was Donovan's wife I found out by reading the stories in the magazines. Fuller was his lawyer.

I am able to trace many of the names my hand writes to Donovan's past.

But there are a score of others as if his memory is swept by a whirlwind of faces.

NOVEMBER 5

To test whether it still has power over me at a distance, I tried leaving the brain by itself today while I drove toward Phoenix.

After fifteen miles from the house I was summoned by the brain. I turned and drove back to my house at top speed.

This incident proved a new fact. The brain is aware of what I am doing even at a great distance.

It could not know where I had gone, but it was sure I was not in the room or in the house.

I assume that the relative strength of the microvolts generated by my brain tells Donovan whether I am present.

But this is a nebulous theory. Only one conclusion is to be relied on, the empiric proof, which itself is limited as the matter concerned is unknown.

NOVEMBER 6

THE brain discharges approximately 3,500 microvolts.

I do not know how much more new substance will attach itself to the brain; there must be a limit. Or is it theoretically boundless like a cancerous growth?

NOVEMBER 10

SCHRATT entered the laboratory today while the brain was ordering me to write. I heard him speak, but I did not turn my head to answer. I do not want to sever the fine thread which connects me with the brain.

My left hand, like that of a child learning to write, slowly formed words.

Schratt called my name again and, when I did not answer, stopped hesitantly, in the middle of the room. At first he thought he was interrupting some train of thought. Then, alarmed at my strange behavior, he stepped closer and looked over my shoulder.

I continued to scrawl words on the paper. For the fifth time I wrote Hinds's name. Then I began to spell: California Merchants Bank. Then the name Hinds appeared again.

Schratt became alarmed. He bent forward to look into my face, which was hidden from him as I sat hunched over the table. A good doctor, he was careful not to touch me for fear of shocking me.

He took the small mirror from the wall and, holding it in front of me, looked into my eyes. He saw I was in a trance. My eyeballs rolled, my mouth twitched. I seemed unaware of his presence.

The brain discontinued its orders. I moved again. Schratt put down the mirror and asked, half fearfully: "Didn't you hear me?"

I nodded.

"Why didn't you answer?"

I shoved toward him the paper covered with the childish scrawls of the brain's dictation. He stared at it and his eyes shifted in fear to the glass vessel.

"I have contacted it," I explained. "Or rather it has contacted me."

I described everything I had experienced, glad to be able to talk to someone about it. He would understand, I thought, but Schratt grew more than alarmed. His bloated face became livid and he shook his head in despair.

I made a last attempt to reason with him.

"Why can't you rid yourself of your inhibitions?" I asked. "Human emotions should have no part in scientific research. They obscure our observations. We cannot permit ourselves to be afraid. Reason, observation, and courage make the scientist, but you seem to lack at least two of these essentials."

"Don't be facetious," Schratt retorted laboredly. "We have debated too long about the right and wrong of this experiment. I beg you now to stop while it is still in your power to stop. Please, Patrick—turn off the pump and let the brain die!"

Suddenly tears ran down his cheeks; his huge body shook with his uncontrollable emotion. It was a disgusting sight. He was growing more helpless and senile every day.

I stepped over to the work table and busied myself with some instruments. I did not turn around when he left the laboratory.

NOVEMBER 11

I HAD fallen asleep exhausted, my strength and nervous energy drained by the double life I am leading.

A wailing, muffled shout echoed in my dream and woke me. It came from the living-room. The cry rose to an insane shriek as if someone was losing his mind from fear. I had never heard the voice before.

I jumped to the door. The bulb flickered as if the brain was shaken by the strange commotion too. As I ran past the vessel, I switched on the encephalograph to be able to study the brain's reaction later.

The insane scream was silenced as fast as it had risen. A scuffling noise replaced it, as if a big body was rolling across the floor, upsetting the furniture.

I switched on the living-room light and saw Schratt's heavy body on the carpet. His own thick fingers around his throat were strangling him. His rattled breathing, his red face, and his protruding eyes showed he was suffocating.

I tried to loose his grip at his throat, but I could not unbend the fingers.

Unexpectedly, while I was still working over Schratt's body, a hand wheeled me about and I stared into Franklin's frightened face. Surprised by his attack, I struck out to defend myself and Franklin stumbled, protecting his face with his arms.

I turned back to Schratt, who had fainted. His hands had fallen limply to his sides. I ordered Franklin to help me lift him onto the couch.

Schratt's pulse had nearly doubled its normal beat, his

heart was pounding heavily, and I was afraid he might die of a stroke. I quickly opened his collar and shirt and ordered Franklin to bring some ice.

When Franklin returned with the ice bag, I put it over Schratt's heart. Soon the extreme palpitation slowed and the pulse came back to normal. Schratt sighed and opened his eyes. He stared at me in terror. I spoke soothingly and forced him to swallow some milk, but his teeth chattered so he spilled half of it.

Schratt had been in the act of leaving. His luggage stood near the door, and his coat lay on a chair. I was puzzled at his sneaking away by night. I could not figure out why he had come through the house at all when the nearest way from his room was by the garden.

"What's the idea?" I asked, pointing to the luggage.

I stood up and Schratt's features froze in terror. I could not make out what ailed him; it was no cataleptic fit. Then I followed his gaze and understood.

The fuse box for the house and the laboratory had been pried open. Schratt's hat lay on the floor near it.

I suddenly understood and a cold murderous rage gripped me.

"You wanted to kill the brain!" I shouted. I nearly lost control of myself.

He stared at me. I had frightened him more.

"You tried to strangle me," he said, his mouth quivering. I had never seen him so out of control.

I was shocked. He thought *I* had attacked him.

Quietly and precisely I explained how I had found him. I actually had saved him from committing suicide!

"Nobody can strangle himself," Schratt said scornfully. "You know that is impossible, Patrick."

Schratt got up and stood on trembling legs.

"I'll see you in the morning," he croaked.

When I tried to help him, he refused my aid.

I returned to the laboratory. The bulb was dark, the brain asleep. The encephalogram showed extremely irregular delta waves.

I sat down to reconstruct the accident.

That shout for help had wakened me. I could clearly remember the sound of the voice, and it did not seem to have been Schratt's. Still, it is very difficult to recognize a voice which is strangled with terror. It must have been Schratt's. Whose else could I have heard?

To dispel a suspicion—the consequences of which were too complex for me to follow up now—I went to Franklin's room.

He was throwing his few belongings into a battered old suitcase. My appearance seemed to frighten him.

His sudden decision to leave me after so many years of service made me more doubtful of myself.

"You leaving too, Franklin? In the middle of the night?" I asked.

Franklin slowly sat down on the bed, watching me with the same helpless terror Schratt had displayed.

To put Franklin at ease, I told him he was free to leave any time he liked, but I should regret it very much. He calmed down a little and I asked if he had heard Dr. Schratt calling for help.

To my relief, he nodded. But when I asked why he had dragged me away from Schratt, he frightenedly confessed he had found me attacking him.

"Dr. Schratt was having a cataleptic fit," I answered curtly. "I was only helping him."

Franklin nodded, but I could see he did not believe me, and when I went back to the laboratory, I felt upset and uneasy.

I tried to unravel the complications. Franklin too had heard Schratt's cries for help. He had pulled me away so vigorously I still felt the pain of his grip on my shoulder. He would never have dared to touch me except in an emergency.

A man cannot strangle himself.

Schratt was right in stating the absurdity of what I had said. It seemed beyond doubt that I had attacked him.

Has the brain reached such strength it can order me to kill? If it has, what is the limit of its power? As human energy in a moment of mortal danger rises to its highest peak, it is conceivable that the brain, spending all its resources, called me to its rescue.

It was aware of Schratt's decision to cut off the electricity. The machinery and the electric circuit are as vital to the brain's existence as heart and lungs to a normal being. When Schratt approached the fuse box, the brain felt itself threatened.

We understand scarcely any of the unpredictable phenomena of human brain-power. We only know that electric potentials travel through the billion cells which form the gray matter of the brain.

Isolated cells have the faculty of producing new ones, whose functions are unknown. Their purpose cannot be explained by our present concepts.

While I slept, my receptor neurons received a strong stimulus from Donovan's nervous center. Its potential, increased by the new cells, was strong enough to influence the motor neurons and to compel me to come to its rescue. Only when Franklin pulled me back, I woke from my murderous dream.

The brain could not influence Schratt, for he was not asleep as I was. This leads to the conclusion that the brain can command only persons who are asleep or willing to submit.

The voice I heard in my dream was Donovan's, inaudible except to the secret ear of my mind.

NOVEMBER 12

SCHRATT came into the laboratory at noon. He looked rested, had shaved carefully, and wore an expression of youthful determination that surprised me.

To my further surprise, he greeted me with a smile.

"Franklin has deserted. We'll have to get used to each other's cooking," he said gaily.

Deliberately I talked of last night and of my regret at having attacked him while under the influence of Donovan's brain. I promised to prevent a repetition of such an occurrence.

He nodded soberly, seemingly without misgiving, and excused himself for having tried to interfere with the experiment.

Suddenly he enlarged on the unlimited possibilities of

my researches. He congratulated me on their success as demonstrated last night and added jokingly that he saw me getting the Nobel prize soon.

I could not account for this sudden change of attitude.

I explained the misadventure by elucidating my theory of the brain's new powers. Pointing out the new cell formation which had twisted the brain out of shape, I stated my convinction that the telepathic power might have its source there.

Schratt agreed with me and, rationalizing his sudden change of attitude, he said: "I had a bad night, Patrick, but I deserved it. I had no right to interfere with your researches. I'm getting old and wacky, and repentful as an old whore. You have your genius and you'd be a fool not to use it to capacity. Envy made me fight you. Forgive a jealous old man."

I still could not see the reason for his sudden change of attitude, but I took it at face value, glad to have him for a collaborator as I had always wished.

Especially since Franklin had left for good.

NOVEMBER 21

I AM at the Roosevelt Hotel in Los Angeles.

Schratt has taken over the job of nursing the brain. He was so enthusiastic about his duties, he silenced my apprehensions.

I can trust him to record the brain's reactions minutely. I will talk to him every day by phone.

Before I decided to leave Washington Junction I got in touch with the brain by Morse and signaled it my decision.

I have trained myself to receive its reply at once. I can make my mind blank and completely receptive.

The brain seemed eager for me to go. What the purpose of my journey is I do not know yet, but the command to go was clear.

The same dream had haunted me for nights, and I am sure it contained the message Donovan wants me to communicate.

Donovan never saw me, for he was in a coma when I found him. Consequently, the brain cannot picture me and

I did not actually see myself in the dream. Since the brain is unable to receive new visual impressions, it must rely on its memory, and in its memory I do not exist.

But Donovan knew the California Merchants Bank. In my dream I entered and walked over to the teller, a sallow-faced man with a small mustache. I asked for a blank check, stepped to a desk, filled out the form for a huge sum, and signed the check with the name of Roger Hinds, of whom I have never heard. Before I took the check to the cashier, I drew an ace of spades in the upper right-hand corner.

The dream repeated itself without a single variation, like a story told for a child to remember.

When I woke I always found on my desk a paper with a crudely drawn map of Los Angeles on which some of the streets and the Merchants Bank were plainly marked.

The message was clear enough, but it did not make sense. I asked Schratt's advice and he urged me to leave at once.

I stood at a crossroad in my work. If I took orders from the brain, I, no longer the scientific observer, would be practically a tool.

The brain could not force me to go. My free will was not impaired yet, and I was still strong enough to refuse this fragment of living tissue which I was cultivating in a glass respirator.

Once Donovan had almost compelled me to murder, but an eruption of force could not be produced at will. It was generated by most extraordinary circumstances.

My money was running low. I found a few hundred dollars Janice had left for me and gave them to Schratt. I was acting for the brain according to a plan which had been conceived in its inert matter.

Since its experience had stopped at the moment of the plane crash, it must be carrying out some plan it had nursed since before the accident.

NOVEMBER 22

THIS morning I had an annoying interference. I was ready to leave the hotel for the bank when the clerk informed me that a Mr. Yocum urgently wanted to see me. I did not know anybody by that name, but I said to have the man wait for me in the lobby.

As soon as I came down in the elevator, I recognized Yocum. He was the shabby photographer who had taken my picture outside the Phoenix hospital. The man was pretending not to see me. He had an old leather briefcase under his arm. When the clerk pointed him out to me, he came over quickly and stood so close he almost touched me.

"Dr. Cory?" he asked in a hoarse voice.

He stared at me as if he hoped to intimidate me, but when I stared back, his gaze dropped.

I was sure he had planned this entrance carefully, but he lacked courage to carry the scene through. His whole appearance was that of a man unstable in his emotions, shaken by fear. I could tell he was up to something and his anxiety betrayed his desire to carry out the plan.

I did not speak. I kept on staring at him. Neurotics soon lose courage. It was obvious that he needed money. He had been on my trail ever since the accident, taking photographs at the hospital, spying on me and my household. Suddenly I guessed what he was after. He had photographed Donovan in the morgue and examined the bandages.

My concern must have shown in my face for he suddenly found his courage again and said: "Could I see you alone?"

We walked into the cocktail bar and sat down.

"I took a picture of you in Phoenix. Here it is," he began nervously, opening his brief-case.

His fingers, long, thin, and stained with tobacco, held the photo in front of me. I did not look at it. I waited silently. Again he lost his poise and for a minute nothing was said.

"I don't care to buy the picture." I finally spoke and my words gave him a cue.

He nodded and quickly drew another photo from the brief-case.

This one was of Donovan in the morgue. I could not help looking at it. Donovan's face had grown dim in my memory and, seeing it, I was intrigued to identify those features with the brain I had learned to know so intimately.

Yocum watched my obvious interest with growing boldness.

"I knew you'd like it," he said with an expression which alarmed me. "And here is one which will really interest you."

He had photographed Donovan's head without bandages. The skull was lifted up and the cotton wool I had stuffed into the cranium was visible. It was a good clear job of photography.

For a moment I was too shocked to move. Then I picked up the picture and turned it face down on the table.

"You can have the negative," Yocum proposed quietly. As I leaned forward he stood up quickly, afraid I might strike him. I managed to look impassive.

"I don't want it. What would I do with it?" I asked. He smiled, but his chin trembled. He had been working himself up to this moment so long. He wanted money. It seemed actually within his reach.

Obviously he needed it badly. His suit was shiny and the shirt front beneath it nothing but a starched dickey. When he moved I saw he was naked inside his coat.

He grew pale as he saw how I stood there just smiling. His eyes, red and hungry and deep-sunk in his gaunt face, glared desperately.

"Who gave you permission to photograph the body?" I asked.

He did not answer, but, sitting down again, he said passionately: "Donovan's family would pay a big price for this. They'll be interested in knowing you stole W. H.'s brain!"

I leaned back in my chair, shocked by his outburst. What did he know about Donovan's brain?

"And here is another one," he said with relish. He felt he had me in a corner now, and he enjoyed the advantage.

He put the picture on the table. It had been photographed through the window of my laboratory at night. He used a flash bulb; the vessel and electric apparatus showed up clearly. He had touched up the picture with a brush and marked the brain.

Yocum sighed and licked a film of saliva across his lips. The typical neurotic, he had maneuvered himself into a spot where he could not back out without losing his skin.

I wondered what Donovan would have done with this desperate imbecile. I was not used to dealing with blackmailers, and the fool might ruin my whole experiment.

There was no use trying to buy him off. If I got the negatives, he would go to Donovan's family with other prints. He was not going to miss any tricks. His single-mindedness increased the danger. His type stops at nothing.

I had no money.

"How much do you want for the negatives?" I asked.

He grinned and nervously touched a dirty handkerchief to his lips.

"Five thousand dollars."

I got up. He hugged his brief-case close to him. His eyes were pleading. He had lost all his air of assurance and was only pitiful.

"All right," I said. "But I don't have that much money on me. And you don't want a check."

If I could stall him off for a day I might find a way out. Donovan had to do something to save us. If only I could get in touch with him!

"You'll find me at the Ontra Cafeteria, Hollywood and Vine, at eight tonight," he said, looking past me with an expression of mingled sullenness and excitement.

Abruptly he turned and walked away, his shoulders hunched up to his ears.

Two hundred miles from Washington Junction and my laboratory, I suddenly felt incapable of the task which had been set for me. It presented seemingly unsurmountable difficulties now.

I sat down in one of the soft chairs in the lobby and tried to organize a campaign. When I closed my eyes, I felt creeping upon me the strange sensation that always preceded the brain's messages.

My mind dimmed and though I could still recognize my own thoughts, they were hidden behind a transparent screen, cut off from my full consciousness.

I felt a strong urge to get up. Obediently I rose and left the hotel, walking down the street, stopping for traffic signals, moving perfunctorily, guided by Donovan's will.

I did not resist the powerful impulse which propelled me.

Donovan's brain did not vacillate. It was closed to new impressions, shut off from new ideas, which flow across the ordinary mind in an unending stream, always to distract it.

Donovan's brain was thinking straight and to the point, the one point only. Its single thought propelled me.

I stopped at the California Merchants Bank, which I had seen in my dream. I pushed open the door and walked over to the teller, who, as I had visioned him, was sallow-faced and black-mustached. I asked for a blank check, stepped back to the writing-desk, and picked up a pen in my left hand.

I filled out the check to cash, fifty thousand dollars, signed the name Roger Hinds in Donovan's handwriting, and carefully drew an ace of spades in the upper right-hand corner.

Not for a moment did I doubt that the cashier would give me the money. He picked up the check, then looked startled.

"Mr. Hinds?" he asked.

"In big bills," I answered, disregarding the question.

"Please endorse the check yourself on the back, sir," he said, to find out my name.

I wrote Patrick F. Cory in my own handwriting.

He stared at it irresolutely.

"Make it big bills," I heard myself repeat as the man disappeared with a murmured excuse.

The policeman at the door moved forward to keep an eye on me. I knew I must have aroused his suspicion, but still not the slightest apprehension, nor even the thought of preparing an explanation, entered my mind.

It was Donovan who acted. I was perfectly at ease, let him take care of everything.

"The manager wants to see you, Mr. Cory." The man with the mustache had come back and was leading me over to a small office.

A bald-headed man sat behind a brown desk. He got up, muttered his name, and asked: "Mr. Hinds?"

"I am Patrick Cory, M.D.," I said, and the man turned over the check and nodded. He offered me a chair, waited in silence till the door opened again, and another man entered.

"This is Mr. Mannings, Dr. Cory."

The newcomer had the unmistakable look of a private detective. We shook hands.

"Would you mind answering a few questions, Dr. Cory?"

"Is anything wrong with the check?" I asked.

The manager looked at the detective, but at the same time answered my question with a nod.

"No. We have compared this signature with the original signature of Mr. Hinds. It is the same, undoubtedly. Also the sign in the corner proves it, the ace of spades. Mr. Hinds demanded that only checks so marked be honored."

He was speaking quickly, eager to convince himself he was not making a mistake.

"If you made out the check yourself, you must be Mr. Hinds and not Dr. Cory," the detective entered the conversation.

Instead of answering, I put my doctor's credentials down in front of him.

"Am I obliged to inform you about my private affairs?" I asked quietly.

"Of course not," the manager hastened to assure me. "Only this account was opened under extraordinary circumstances."

He waited for me to say something, but when I sat silent, he continued: "We received quite a large sum of money and a letter from Mr. Hinds, who did not give us his address and is unknown to us with the request that we open an account for him. A commercial account. No interest."

He stressed the fact that he found it strange for so large a sum to be deposited where it would earn no interest. It was against his business principles.

"That was nearly twelve years ago. Now the first check is drawn against the account, and you have signed it. If you are not Mr. Hinds, we would be happy to receive some information about the gentleman, because," he smiled wanly, "the bank likes to know the clients it is serving."

"You mean in case of stolen money?" I asked.

"Oh no. We know what bank the notes came from. We always check on that." The manager spoke with professional pride. "But Mr. Hinds . . ."

"I am Dr. Cory. Will you please cash the check now? I am in a hurry!" I got up.

The manager rose too, distressed.

"You're within your legal rights, Dr. Cory, not to answer questions," the detective said, but there was a hidden threat in his voice.

Half an hour later I walked out of the bank with my pockets bulging with money. What should I do with it? Pay the blackmailer?

I bought a brief-case, stuffed the money into it, and went back to the hotel. I felt tired as always when the brain had communicated with me. I went upstairs to rest and wait for further orders.

Janice was in town. She had left a message for me to ring her at Cedars of Lebanon Hospital. Schratt had told her where I was staying.

I was at a loss to understand what the brain intended to do. To all appearances it had prepared itself to meet Yocum's demand or it would not have sent me to the bank. The brain seemed to want me to pay Yocum and get the negatives, but still I had received no definite order.

Lying on my bed in the hotel room waiting for Donovan to communicate with me, I felt that I had reached the borderline of sanity, beyond which the firm rational ground falls away from under our feet.

I picked up the phone to call Schratt, but I must have asked for the hospital, because Cedars of Lebanon answered. Since I was connected anyway, I asked for Janice.

When I heard her voice, distant and full of happy surprise, I suddenly felt calm.

Promising Janice to see her one day soon, I quickly hung up.

I had to meet Yocum, and after that I would go back home to continue the research myself. There was nothing to gain by staying away from the brain longer. I knew now that distance did not lessen its influence, and with this proved, the purpose of my journey was achieved.

I told the clerk I was checking out next day. Then I opened the brief-case and put half the money into my pockets. Yocum had said five thousand dollars, he might ask for more. I did not care how much I paid him. It was not my money and I wanted to get rid of it.

I had never had so much money in my hands before, but it was just so much paper to me. My sense of property was limited to the instruments I used in my laboratory. Janice bought and took care of all the rest—my suits, shirts, shoes, our food, the house.

I had fifty thousand dollars in my pocket belonging to a character named Roger Hinds. Did he exist at all, or was this a secret account Donovan had kept for some purpose I could not guess?

Why had Donovan sent me for fifty thousand dollars when the blackmailer only asked five?

I left the brief-case with the rest of the money in the hotel safe and went out.

I was curious as to how Donovan treated blackmailers. He must have had plenty of experience. His success was built on fraud, threat, bribery, and foul play. This little man should present no great problem to him.

I walked down Hollywood Boulevard toward Vine. It was eight o'clock and Donovan had not told me what to do.

When I arrived at the cafeteria, a big place crowded with people, I was still at a loss what to say to Yocum. For a few minutes I walked up and down at the entrance, hoping for advice, but no command reached me.

Perhaps the brain was asleep. Should I telephone Schratt and ask him to wake it?

"Dr. Cory?" a voice whispered behind me.

It was Yocum. He clutched his brief-case close to his chest, and even by the yellow light that shone through the bright windows of the restaurant I could see that his cheeks were flushed with fever.

He led me to a shabby car in the parking lot next to the cafeteria. It had a California license plate with a very easy number to remember.

He moved his lips in a soundless attempt to talk. I could tell he had tuberculosis of the throat; the glottal ligaments were affected already and his voice had given out. But in his excitement he was unaware that I could not hear him.

I took the money from my pocket and he dropped his case to grab the notes with both hands.

I picked up the brief-case and opened it. Three negatives and some prints were in it, wrapped in newspaper.

Yocum made no other attempt to talk. He stepped into his car, slammed the door, and rolled up the window. He smiled at me, showing big yellow teeth, moved his lips again, and drove off.

As soon as he had left, I stepped into a taxi. Donovan

had called it. In an excited voice I ordered the driver to follow the small yellow coupé, but I could not figure out what the brain purposed by pursuit.

Yocum drove his car down the boulevard, weaving in and out of traffic. Brakes shrieked and cars skidded to a stop.

"That guy will get a ticket!" the driver called back through the window.

We drove up Laurel Canyon, but the yellow coupé had disappeared. At Kirkwood Drive, having lost Yocum, I dismissed the taxi and walked on, climbing the grade.

I was not following a plan, just leaving it to Donovan to show me where to go. Up an unpaved road, deeply rutted with rain, I discovered Yocum's car, it's door open, parked at the bottom of a small hill. A hundred feet farther a ramshackle hut was half hidden behind tall eucalyptus trees.

I climbed the hill and peered through the window of the cottage. In the middle of a dirty room stood Yocum, in front of a fireplace stuffed with rubbish, old paper, and discarded photographs. In one corner a mattress was covered with torn blankets. There were a couple of kitchen chairs and a table. The windows were so dirty they looked paint-smeared.

Yocum was acting very strangely. He had carefully spread the bank notes over the floor and had taken off his shoes. He was walking on the money in his stocking feet, careful not to disarrange it.

He stomped like an ostrich, lifting his feet high. Then he jumped into the air, hit the floor again with knees bent, and balanced there, elbows lifted, hands dropped like a big bird flapping its wings. All the time he uttered little cries, ululating to himself, his eyes glowing in feverish ecstasy.

Believing himself alone, he followed his neurotic trauma.

I pushed the door open. Yocum froze in his tracks, then fell on his knees and grabbed the money.

He turned toward me, his mouth hanging open with fright, stepped behind the table, and pressed the money to his chest. The tattered dickey he wore slid aside and showed his bony thorax.

"What do you want?" he asked hoarsely. He had got his voice back.

"The other negatives," I said, "and the rest of the prints."

Yocum retreated, alarmed, into a corner of the room.

"I have no other negatives," he said dully, but he was sizing me up.

"Five thousand more if you hand over everything you have," I said.

His chin began to tremble and he leaned against the wall for support.

"Ten thousand," he said slowly.

"Then there are other negatives!" I stepped closer and he retreated at once.

On the mantelpiece lay matches and an old pipe with a much bitten stem. I lighted a match and threw it into the fireplace. The paper and photos flared up.

Yocum stared at me, pertified. He did not dare run past me, though he was crazy to get out of the room.

"You can take everthing for five," he stammered.

The fire, fed by the celluloid on the photoprints, roared brightly. With one foot I kicked a hunk of flame onto the rug-covered mattress.

When Yocum jumped forward to pass me, I grabbed him by his thin neck and dragged him to the door. The money fluttered out of his hands. He did not try to fight; paralyzed by fear, he simply collapsed in my hands. His voice left him again and he screamed soundlessly with wide-open mouth.

I pulled him out of the house, his feet dragging in the dust. Behind me I heard the crackling of the flames, devouring the old shack.

I walked on, yanking Yocum behind me. I stuffed him into the car, slid behind the wheel, and drove off.

At the bottom of Kirkwood Drive I turned left and followed the road up Laurel Canyon. Distant fire sirens shrieked and a white pall of smoke drifted up over the canyon.

At the intersection of Laurel and Mulholland Drive I had to stop to let some fire engines pass. Then I slowly drove the car up a dirt road.

Yocum did not move. His bony head had dropped onto his knees.

When he finally lifted his face, he looked punch-drunk. "You burned the money," he whispered.

I stared at the valley below me, at the mountains behind Burbank. Suddenly I was uneasy. Donovan had stopped giving me orders and I was on my own.

"All my life I wanted a little money," Yocum murmured. "Now you've burned it."

His despair overcame his fear and he began to accuse me.

"Look at me. Rotting away." He opened his dirty coat to show his fleshless body. "I don't want to die. I wanted to live for once, and you burned my money!"

He did not remember that he had blackmailed me. The money had been in his grasp and to take it away from him was robbery.

Sliding out of the car, he stood tottering at the edge of the embankment. He was at the end of his rope.

"I'm thirty-eight," he murmured, bending over me as if accusing me with these words. "I haven't had a decent meal in years! I have to have money now! I can't get it by working; I'm sick and they don't want a man who coughs and loses his voice. They want them healthy and strong. Not like me!"

He stared at me. His eyes were colorless.

"Just once I got a break when I had typhoid and they kept me in a hospital for three months. They put me with twenty other guys, but still I had a whopping good time. Somebody to feed me, somebody to look after me. I kept thinking how nice it would be to be sick alone in a room, with a bell to ring for the nurse and everything quiet if I wanted to be quiet. Can't be so bad to die first-class. I've been thinking of it for years!"

He grinned, baring his stained teeth. It seemed to give him pleasure to tell me his misery.

"When Donovan cracked up, I got the scoop. The only photographer in Phoenix! And how much did they give me? Ten bucks! I could have held out for more but they knew I needed money. And when they know you need money, they'll pay you a dime for a gold nugget!"

He seemed to be pleased that life had been consistently cruel.

"I photographed Donovan's empty skull to show how he was killed. I had no plan when I made the shot. Maybe they always take out dead men's brains, I wouldn't have known. Then I took pictures of your house and your wife and your car. I got one shot through the window of your laboratory, and when I enlarged the photo, I saw the thing swimming in the glass bowl. It looked like Donovan's missing brain to me. I put two and two together and knew you were up to something. They don't just casually take out people's brains and dump them into goldfish bowls!"

He laughed at me as if the joke pleased him.

"Then I found out everything about you. You didn't have much money, but when I trailed you here and saw you go into the bank, you stuffed bills into that brief-case. It wasn't very smart to carry all that around. I had asked for five thousand and I could just as well have said a million, but what difference would it have made? When I had the money you burned it!"

He sobbed, but he had no tears left. His mouth hung open and the sound strangled into a croak.

Now I was sure I had burned all the rest of the prints and negatives. I stepped out of the car and he was afraid I might leave him there with his car on Mulholland. When hope ends, the world ends too.

He may have been an honest man all his life only because he was convinced that if things were ever too bad, he could be dishonest and change his luck. Now that this had not worked out either, he despaired. Every experience of his confirmed his pessimism about the world he knew, and he had lost his foolish optimism about the world he had not lived in. He was disillusioned.

"You burned my camera too!" he said. "A Graflex. Seventy-five dollars second-hand. It took me a year to pay for it."

He was coming down to earth; his misery had focused on concrete facts. He had lost a camera. The five thousand dollars was dream money. The camera was real.

He was going to die soon. I did not give him more than six months. Why shouldn't he die on Donovan's money? I took a bundle of bank notes from my pocket and passed it to him. I held out the notes and I felt no interference. Donovan did not object.

Yocum stared at the money in my hand, not daring to touch it.

"Buy yourself a golden camera. Rent a room in a sanitarium," I said. "Get yourself into shape again!"

He took the bills and moved his lips convulsively.

I walked away. I preferred to hike the mile down to Ventura Boulevard rather than be embarrassed by his sentimental outburst.

A cab on Wilson Drive took me back to the hotel.

I phoned Schratt before I packed to leave for Washington Junction, to tell him I was on the way. The operator had to ring several times before there was an answer.

"I was asleep," Schratt explained, but his voice sounded wide awake. "How are you, Patrick?"

I told him I would be home next day. He indicated no enthusiasm; I had the impression my return embarrassed him. I was afraid something had gone wrong with the brain.

"Oh no," Schratt answered hastily. "Everything is fine. I just measured the electric discharge. It increases rapidly in output, close to five thousand microvolts now. The brain has grown twice its original size, too. If this continues, we shall have to have a bigger flask. I have enough brain ash for the serum. You needn't worry, Patrick!"

He was very eager to dispel my uneasiness, but did not encourage me to return. He wanted me to stay in Los Angeles and go wherever the brain told me to. He talked as if he were carrying out the experiment and I were the apprentice.

"But there is no reason to stay here." I was surprised to find myself on the defensive. "I have found out everything I wanted to know. No use hunting down facts I already have."

Schratt objected as glibly as if he had thought this out in advance:

"But you still don't know why Donovan ordered you to Los Angeles! Is the brain's thinking logical or not? Have you found out whether it works according to a preconceived plan? Are its orders just a blurred outburst, void of reason, or is it proceeding systematically toward a fixed

71

conclusion? I think you are obliged to find out whether this apparently exuberant growth of cell tissues destroys the organized process of thinking or augments it. Only then you will know whether the brain alone can carry out the process of thought or the whole central nervous system is interdependent."

I was at a loss to answer. Schratt had swamped me with questions. His feverish interest puzzled me and I could not dismiss the suspicion that he assumed this urgency to keep me away.

"By the way," he went on, "how is Janice? Did you see her? She is at Cedars of Lebanon."

"I've talked to her," I answered, "but haven't seen her yet."

"You ought to," he said. This time there was honest concern in his voice.

"I may," I answered, "but even so, I'll be back tomorrow." He had nothing to reply. We hung up.

It was close to midnight, but before I went to bed I put a pad and pencil within reach. I was drowsy. The street noises grew dim. Someone in the next room was talking on the phone, but soon his voice lost its animation and his words grew meaningless.

In the half dream which dulled my mind I repeated a name I had heard somewhere before: Anton Sternli. The thought ran in circles in my half consciousness and followed me into my sleep.

NOVEMBER 28

TODAY for the first time in a week I am able to continue my record. The night after I burned Yocum's shack I did not dream of anything so far as I can remember, but Schratt's voice repeated a single sentence, unendingly. The phrase made no sense to me, but all the time it echoed in my sleep, a terror gripped me as if the words were a threat of mortal danger. "Amidst the mists and coldest frosts he thrusts his fists against the posts and still insists he sees the ghost."

Unmistakably it was Schratt's voice that spoke again and again: It followed me into the day.

I got up. On the floor I found a message I had written in the night. Anton Sternli, Pasadena, 120 Byron Street, was clearly put down in Donovan's handwriting.

"Five hundred dollars," I had written after the name, and following it the number: 142235.

I dressed and went out to find that man.

He did not live at 120 Byron Street, but at 210. That proved that Donovan's memory is not infallible. He can make mistakes like an ordinary human being.

When I rang the bell, a young girl of fourteen opened the door. I asked for Mr. Sternli and she let me into a small library where an old man, bent and white-haired, sat alone.

He was so nearly blind, his eyes could not focus me, but he did not wear glasses. He looked vaguely in the direction from which my voice came, groping along the desk as he rose to move toward me.

"I am Dr. Cory," I said. "W. H. Donovan sent me."

My words had a curious effect. He stopped in his tracks. His sightless eyes shifted nervously.

"Mr. Donovan is dead," he answered uneasily.

"Of course," I said. "He died in my house at Washington Junction."

Sternli asked me to sit down and felt his way back to the desk.

"What can I do for you, doctor?" he asked.

"Donovan told me to get in touch with you. He wanted me to bring you five hundred dollars."

I took the money from my pocket and put it on the table, but Sternli was too near-sighted to see my motion. He looked toward me irritatedly, as if he had not understood, then repeated: "Five hundred dollars."

I got up and laid down the money in front of him. He bent down to peer at it. Suddenly he smiled and said in a humorous tone: "It comes just in time. As a matter of fact, money always comes in time or too late, but never too soon. I have broken my glasses and could hardly afford new ones. They are very expensive; I am nearly blind."

He picked up a broken lens from his desk and looked through it toward me.

"You don't mind if I stare at you like this? It is all that is left. I sat on them!"

He chuckled ruefully.

We sat silent until he questioned in a kind voice: "W. H. thought of me before he died? Then I certainly misjudged him all his life."

He shook his head and carefully put down the fragment of glass. "What else did he tell you?"

"Nothing. He was in no condition to talk."

"He did not tell you who I am?" he asked. At once, not to embarrass me, he added: "I was Mr. Donovan's secretary for many years. To be more precise, during all the years a man can work to provide for his old age."

The room was poorly furnished, except for the rows of expensive books carefully arranged on sturdy shelves. The walls were dingy with age.

"Didn't he leave you any compensation?" I asked politely.

Sternli smiled and nodded.

"The memories of interesting times, yes. But money? No! He never would! That's why I am surprised he thought of me at a moment when every man should think of himself. Death was the last word that could be mentioned in Mr. Donovan's presence. We spoke of it only once and he said: 'Making a will is resigning life. Better not get the idea in your head at all, or it bores into your consciousness like termites in a house. They eat away in secret until one day when you least expect it, the roof crashes onto you. Never mention death to me!' "

Sternli turned his face toward me and I saw he was not so old as I had thought. He could not be more than fifty, but his erudite appearance, his gentle manner, his white hair, made him look twenty years older.

"How can I serve you, Dr. Cory?" he asked.

I hesitated, but my curiosity got the upper hand.

"Well, could you tell me something about Roger Hinds?"

He looked up sharply, a strange look in those myopic eyes that did not focus; then he smiled.

"Roger Hinds is the name W. H. used on a bank account," he said. "I deposited money to it. I even remember the amount of the first deposit. Eighteen hundred thirty-three dollars and eighteen cents. W. H. always liked my memory for things which do not have much significance."

"You mean Roger Hinds never existed?" I asked.

"I don't know. He may have, but I never saw him and W. H. never corresponded with him. He used to be very interested, however, in everyone named Hinds and collected information about them. I don't know why. One of this family is quite notorious recently. You'll find his name in the headlines. He has been accused of murder. A very cruel case of homicide. It happened the first of August of this year, at nine thirty at night."

He touched his forehead with a thin hand.

"I can never forget anything I read or hear," he said apologetically. "Cyril Hinds! He is in the county jail, if that is of any interest to you."

In that strange conglomeration of reality and the almost supernatural I did not know where my own thinking began and Donovan's commands ended.

"He did not mention Hinds's name," I said truthfully. Sternli looked at me and slowly lifted the piece of broken glass to his eye. I realized I had contradicted myself. Donovan must have talked to me about Hinds, otherwise Sternli could not understand, for I had mentioned the name in the first place.

I got up.

Sternli held out his hand rather timidly. "Thank you, Dr. Cory. It was nice of you to bring me the money. But should we not inform Howard Donovan of this gift? He is the heir and he might object to my receiving it."

The last thing I wanted was to tip off Howard Donavan and his lawyers where the money came from, and I lied: "It does not belong to him. It was in an envelope with your name. Donovan gave it to me before he died."

That did not sound very credible, but there was no way of proving I was lying.

"Thank you so very much," Sternli said. "If I can be of any service to you, please let me know. I have a great deal of leisure, unfortunately."

He took my arm to go to the door with me. I felt suddenly Donovan was trying to get a message through to me.

"I should ask you for the key," I said in the doorway.

Sternli peered at me, surprised I had brought up an important request at the moment of departure.

"The key—what key?" he asked, uneasily.

I took the slip of paper with Sternli's name and the serial number on it out of my pocket and showed it to him. He held the paper so close to his eyes it nearly touched them. When he dropped his hand, his face was flushed with amazement.

"W. H.'s writing," he murmured. He groped his way back into the room and returned with a key. It was small and flat for a safe-deposit box.

Alarmed by the erratic instructions the brain had been giving me, I walked back toward town. Donovan made mistakes; his memory was slipping. The deposit-box number had been written down, but the brain had forgotten to mention the key in its message. It had certainly intended to inform me about it, for the number was pertinent to the key. But something had gone wrong with its process of thinking lately. It had been precise before.

I made a note of the hour and date I had received the instructions the night before the 23rd of November, after midnight. I must ask Schratt if he found irregularities in the brain's reactions at that time. Is the organ sick? Is mental decomposition setting in?

It irritated me that the brain only remembered to complete its message when I was leaving Sternli's house.

Walking along, I crossed a street where road gangs were digging ditches. Machines made a deafening noise, shoveling out dirt and throwing it on a moving band which conveyed it to the trucks.

I did not watch where I walked. Concentrated on Donovan, I was trying to force him to complete instructions concerning the key and code number.

Donovan could get in touch with me any time he chose, but I was still cut off from him. It was only a one-way communication system, but as the brain was growing steadily stronger, it should soon freely receive my thoughts.

I walked in a trance, willing Donovan's brain to hear me, with all the power of concentration I possessed.

Suddenly I heard a shriek of brakes beside me. Instinctively I stopped and stumbled. Something heavy hit my back. The groaning and clatter of the big iron shovel was close to my ears.

As I fell a tremendous wave of fear engulfed me. I lost consciousness.

It was night when I awoke.

Even before I opened my eyes, the faint stench of antiseptics told me I was in a hospital. The brownish walls were familiar. They had taken me to Cedars to Lebanon, where I had worked as an intern.

Janice sat by the bed, motionless, watching me. When I stirred she stepped over to me at once. They had packed my thorax in twenty pounds of plaster. Lying motionless, I examined myself mentally, going over my body inch by inch until I was convinced that this was nothing fatal.

I could move my head a little, bend my fingers, lift my arms.

Janice watched me anxiously. She was not sure yet I was fully conscious, for my eyes were still closed.

"Pain?" she asked in a low voice.

Again I listened to my body. I felt suspended in mid-air, as if my back was not compressed in a plaster cast but supported by gentle hands.

I had a strange sensation of being bodyless.

I could feel no effect of a drug. My head was clear, and my mouth did not have the dry, greenish aftertaste of anæsthesia.

"I don't feel anything," I finally said.

My words alarmed her more than as if I had screamed with pain.

"It's spinal concussion," she said.

I closed my eyes. I ought to be suffering the pains of hell if that diagnosis was right. Janice got up to ring for the doctor, but I stopped her.

"I can move my toes and fingers," I said. "I am not paralyzed. There must be some other reason I have no pain. Did they dope me?"

I knew she would deny it and she did.

"You were in pain while you were unconscious," she said. "For hours. In great pain."

She spoke calmly, submitting to me an observation of symptons, like one doctor to another. She knew enough of medicine to be as surprised and alarmed as I was. Spinal concussion is usually accompanied by pain.

"What happened to me?" I asked.

"The silliest thing," she said cheerfully. "You fell into a ditch in the street and a steam shovel crushed you."

She looked very well, and I noticed that she was attractive in her nurse's white uniform. She had lost that anemic look and I was half convinced she had not really been sick at all. It was our unhappy marriage that had broken her down.

"Is that the outfit they give patients?" I said, looking at her uniform.

"I got permission to come on this case myself."

She spoke with a stubbornness which had grown out of long consideration.

I looked at her face, white and transparent in the yellow light of the lamp behind the screen in the far corner of the room. Her eyes were enormous, dark.

Everything seemed larger than life, everything moved with a slow motion. Shadows and light became one great waving veil. The sheets that covered the cast towered like mountains.

Janice's light hands adjusted them so that I could see the wall opposite.

It was not unpleasant to have her around. I didn't mind if she stayed.

I closed my eyes again.

Then the pains stabbed me.

I tried to shake off the plaster cast, which suddenly weighed like tons of steel. My hands clenched in a cramp and the fingernails buried themselves in the flesh of the palms.

"Codeine!"

I tried to make her understand. I could not hear my voice myself; it was lost in a shattering noise that seemed to come from the direction of my spinal cord and filled my ears with an increasing howl.

I knew that pains like these could not be escaped by flight into unconsciousness. They would penetrate any resolution. I knew that all the while I writhed in the attack the knowledge made my pain more torturous.

Strangely that same senseless phrase underlined the torture. "Amidst the mists and coldest frosts he thrusts his fists against the posts and still insists he sees the ghosts."

The pains disappeared as fast as they had attacked. I saw Janice bending anxiously over me. She wiped the perspiration from my forehead. I was floating again, suspended in soft air. Not a memory of my suffering was left.

The door opened and a doctor entered. A nurse behind him rolled in a table with glasses and instruments.

"Hello," the doctor said with professional cheerfulness. "Still in pain?"

He was filling a hypodermic with morphine.

"Thanks, I don't need it," I said definitely.

The man looked astonished. "The pain can't have stopped so quickly," he said.

"I'm surprised myself," I answered, and looked down the length of my body.

There was nothing I could feel. As if I were only a brain, I was hardly aware of arms or legs, or even my injured back.

"Would you mind testing my nerve reactions?"

He stuck me in the arm with a pin, but I experienced no pain reaction.

I felt like a patient under a spinal anæsthetic.

"Are you sure your diagnosis is right?" I questioned.

He indicated that he was.

I closed my eyes; I wanted to think out clearly what had happened to me. I heard the doctor whisper to Janice and leave.

As soon as he had gone, I asked her to get Schratt on the phone.

She hesitated and I repeated the order.

A few minutes later I was talking to Schratt.

"How are you, Patrick?" he asked, relieved to hear my voice. "Janice told me about the accident."

Janice stood at the window with her back turned.

"I wanted to ask you," I said slowly, prepared for the pain to return any moment, "if the brain has acted differently during the last forty-eight hours."

He did not reply at first.

"I did not want to alarm you as long as you were ill . . ." he said finally, "but it seems to have a fever. I can't make out why. The temperature rises quickly, then drops to normal when it is asleep."

Suddenly the pains attacked me with increased fury. I thought I could not stand them. Even the bones of my skull hurt as if a fist were pushing from inside.

"Wake the brain!" I cried into the phone. "Wake it up! Knock at the glass! Frighten it! Don't let it sleep!"

The receiver dropped out of my hands. I bit my lower lip until blood filled my mouth.

Janice grabbed the hypodermic, but the pain evaporated like steam.

I took the receiver again and heard Schratt come back to the phone.

"The brain is awake now, Patrick. The lamp is burning." Then: "What did it do to you?"

My head sank back on the pillow. I knew what had happened and tried to tell Schratt.

"It suffers my pain when it is awake," I said, controlled. "It suffers the pain instead of me. It seems to have penetrated my thalamus. Its cortex now receives the reflexes of my nervous system. My body's pains are experiences in Donovan's cerebrum. It takes possession of me more and more. Before, it controlled only my motor nerves, but now it dominates that part of my brain where pain registers."

Schratt was breathing so loudly I could hear him.

"If this continues," he said, "it soon will control your will."

"What of it?" I asked, trying to speak lightly. "Some men have given more than their identity to science."

"Yes," he said, and suddenly hung up.

Groping, I put the receiver back on the hook.

"Now I'll be all right," I said to Janice. I forgot she had listened to our conversation. Schratt's voice had been loud enough for her to hear.

Janice stared at me, her eyes wide with terror and despair. I had not known how much she knew, but now, understanding some of the consequences, she divined the abyss of destruction to which the experiment had led me.

During the last few days the pains have bothered me less, but I am still confined to my plaster prison. Even when I get up, I shall have to carry twenty pounds of cast around with me.

The brain has given me some addresses: of one Alfred Hinds, in Seattle, and of a Geraldine Hinds in Reno. It insistently repeated the names last night.

Once, impelled by telepathic command, I tried to get out of bed, but Janice, hearing my moans, gave me a shot of morphine which immediately severed communication with the brain. It was like cutting off a telephone connection. When I am drugged, the brain cannot get in touch with me. It seems at a loss to understand why I do not follow its orders.

It is not aware I have had an accident. I tried to tell Donovan about it. Lying quietly, putting myself in a trance of concentration like a yogi, I tried to transmit the message. I could not.

In my dreams and lately during the day that strange sentence returns again and again: "Amidst the mists and coldest frosts . . ."

Its unending repetition tortures me as much as the pain. There must be some meaning. The brain must have a purpose in repeating it.

I phoned Schratt and told him about it. He seemed amazed when I spoke the sentence to him, but he insisted he had never heard it before.

I asked Janice. Finally, after thinking it over for a day, she came to the conclusion it must be a rhyme to cure people of lisping.

That sounds likely, but why should the brain repeat such a line?

Janice and I avoid mentioning the brain. She is waiting for me to speak first, but I have not the slightest intention of bringing up the subject. She knows too much already; it disturbs me to see her ponder about it. Whatever comes into Janice's mind is written all over her face. She would be the worst secret agent in the world.

But I am getting used again to having her around. Actually during the few hours she leaves me with another nurse in her place I feel uneasy, as if something might happen and only she could help me.

When she is not around I sometimes become sentimental

about her. I recall the day when I was hitch-hiking my way back from Santa Barbara to the hospital and she gave me a lift. How often she waited patiently in her car to chauffeur me around; I had to live on the twenty dollars the hospital paid its interns.

She has always been willing to give me a lift. That seems to be her function in life.

She is patient. She always was. And persistent.

She made up her mind to marry me. She did. She wanted to get me away from Washington Junction—here I am. Now she is waiting to win me back to her.

She knows when to be around and when to leave me alone. She is like a fine voltmeter, recording the slightest variations in current. How much happiness she could give to some people, instead of wasting her strength on me!"

I must talk to her about that one day.

NOVEMBER 29

ANTON STERNLI visited me. He rang up from the reception desk first. Janice answered the phone and stepped out to meet him at the elevator.

She kept him in the corridor nearly an hour, talking to him, before she let him see me.

When we lived on the desert, Janice limited her activities to running our house. Now, taking advantage of my helplessness, she has extended her field to the people connected with me. She has always had Schratt in the palm of her hand, and Sternli has been easy.

Sternli looked more like a Swiss professor than ever when he came into the room, peering at me through heavy glasses that made his eyes look the size of hazelnuts. That suit could never have been made for him; the trousers bagged over his knees. He carried a white cane like a blind man's.

Sternli had seen about my accident in the papers and would have come before, but he only got his glasses yesterday. He wanted to tell me how sorry he was.

He talked about insignificant things until Janice left us.

She had seen in his eager face that he wanted to be alone with me.

"You startled me with that memorandum in Donovan's handwriting," Sternli began. "You see, before he left for Florida he gave me the key and wrote down a number. All his life he was over-cautious about everything. Even when he signed his name, he would shield his left hand with his right so no one could see what he wrote until he had finished. I am astonished he should have thought of me at the hour of his death! And why did he have my name on an envelope with money in it in his pocket? He was never generous unless there was advantage to himself: It makes me uneasy, Dr. Cory."

"You judge him too harshly," I said. I saw complications ahead.

"Oh no."

Sternli took off his glasses and cleaned them studiously with a small piece of chamois, holding them close to his eyes from time to time.

"W. H. was my whole life. How can I hate what I was a part of? When W. H. dismissed me there was nothing left to live for. I have no family, not even a friend. To make friends one must be tolerant and interested, and with advancing age we become less and less adaptable. One has to give to keep friends, and my larder is empty. There are two species of man, the creative and the imitative. I am the latter. And those people are very barren if no inspiration comes from outside."

He spoke quietly. This was his philosophy; he expressed it without bitterness.

"I have been approached by a publishing house to write a book about W. H. They offer me a great sum of money and I need it for the future; my salary was too small for me to save."

Sternli was eager to talk. He sensed that my relation to Donovan was closer than just that of the one disastrous meeting. He could not define the bond between me and his former master, but he felt impelled to talk with me to free many unspoken words.

He never had spoken to Donovan as he did to me. His natural shyness and fear of his master had prevented it.

Still, for years Sternli had hoped in his heart that some day he would find the courage to talk to him as one man to another. Sternli never did.

Now with Donovan's death that hope had died, but speaking to me was like confessing crimes of which, though only as his master's tool, Sternli was somehow the villain.

He told me his life story, typical of a retired, studious fellow like him, secluded from the world.

Sternli had worshipped Donovan to a degree which destroyed his own personality. Donovan had accepted this devotion and, without any qualms, had taken every possible advantage of the man who would not or could not live a life of his own.

In Zürich, where he was studying languages, Sternli met Donovan. When he saw the millionaire for the first time, in the most expensive hotel, of course, the scholar was immediately fascinated by his powerful personality.

That afternoon Sternli had bought himself a cup of coffee at the Baur-au-Lac Hotel, just to see for once how the rich of the world lived. While he was drinking his coffee slowly, Sternli heard Donovan's booming voice calling for a man to translate some wires into Portuguese. He could hear the frightened desk clerk's apologetic reply.

In a rare fit of courage, which marked the turning point of his life, Sternli offered his services.

Donovan kept him around while he stayed in Zürich, and when he left he asked Sternli to accompany him as his secretary. The young man jumped at this opportunity to see the world.

Sternli became Donovan's shadow, intimate to him as a pair of spectacles. He slept next door to Donovan, followed him from conference to conference, from town to town, from country to country, from continent to continent.

Donovan's secretary, letter-writer, interpreter, but never his friend, Sternli grew into his job, became the walking, living memory of the intricate machine which was Donovan's brain.

He never took a holiday; he would not have known what to do with himself. Only once, when his mother was dangerously ill, he asked for a short leave of absence to visit her.

84

Reluctantly Donovan agreed, and when Sternli asked him for money for the trip to Europe, Donovan made him sign a personal note for the five hundred dollars.

In telling this story Sternli skipped over a part of his life. I could only guess at what he wanted to conceal.

He had been in love once. As fate ironically decided, it was with Donovan's wife, Katherine. She must have been a beautiful woman, aloof and unhappy. She did not encourage the shy young man; I assume she never even knew his secret adoration.

One day honest Sternli could not stand the conflict that raged in his conscience. He felt he was not working honestly, and also it seemed disloyal to him to be in love with his employer's wife.

So one day he asked Donovan to release him from his duties.

Donovan immediately offered Sternli a raise. Discontent could always be cured with money. But Sternli wanted to confess.

"You are in love with Katherine!" Donovan said calmly. "What does she say to that?"

Sternli, of course, had never talked to Mrs. Donovan about it. For him, to fall in love with a married woman was a plain violation of one of God's commandments.

"If you haven't told her, there is no reason to quit," Donovan said sanely, and added: "There is no reason to raise your salary either."

With this decision Donovan settled the incident to his own satisfaction. Sternli stayed on. His mind had been made up for him, even in this most intimate and important concern of his life, his love. This made Sternli more dependent than ever.

A few months later Katherine Donovan died.

All the time Sternli was telling me this, he did not give the impression of being a naturally talkative man. He was just relating facts, without so much as a quiver in his voice. Only sometimes, to punctuate a grave revelation, he smiled, took off his glasses, and wiped them carefully.

He·talked on, calmly, unpretentiously. He wanted to get closer to me, and with this story he succeeded in doing so.

I am certain he did not know why he opened his heart to

unreel his life story to a stranger, but slowly his and Donovan's characters gained shape and color. I learned more about Donovan from listening to Sternli's life story than about Sternli himself.

It interested me very much. I had overlooked this obvious approach. Donovan's story as told in the magazines was exaggerated, falsified, yellow-journalized. Here his real self unfolded.

I began to understand the brain's workings. If I could search Donovan's character thoroughly, exploring every emotion of his heart, every reaction of his consciousness, I would understand many of the brain's paradoxes.

I urged Sternli to continue. Like a good psychoanalyst, I tried to read the involvements hidden beneath his words. The parts he unconsciously concealed—because to him they seemed of no importance—I fit together to fill in the gigantic jigsaw puzzle of a powerful man who resolved every pang of conscience and every fit of weakness into a smashing assault on his adversary, as a boxer attacks savagely when he finds himself in a corner.

Sternli's was an idealized picture of Donovan. He was blind to his master's faults. He did not even divine how this man had distorted the pattern of *his* existence, cunningly, patiently, and thoroughly.

It became clear to me that from the moment Sternli confessed a love for Katherine, Donovan had plotted his destruction. Not that Donovan was jealous. He was too big to permit himself that weakness, but somebody had trespassed on his property. Even though the crime was committed only in thought, Donovan felt cheated and robbed.

Sternli told me about Donovan's habit of having people spied on by detectives. Everyone close to him was under secret supervision. Number one of his suspects was Katherine. I was sure Donovan had known every step she took, was informed how she spent every minute of her time. He had checked up on Sternli, too, as a matter of routine. His watchdogs had trailed this little man.

Sternli's eyes got bad. He slowly lost his sight and became unfit to take Donovan's rapid dictation. Another secretary had to be engaged.

Sternli was of no other use than as a living filing system,

an infallible record of things past. Since his usefulness was now cut by half, Donovan logically cut Sternli's salary in half too. And one day he began to collect the five hundred dollars he had advanced years before—in five- and ten-dollar installments out of Sternli's curtailed salary.

When Sternli found himself hard-pressed, Donovan acted surprised.

"Don't tell me you have no money! You must be rich!" he said. "You must have made enough on the side."

Sternli, deeply hurt, defended himself.

"I am not insinuating you filched coins from my pocket," Donovan said. "But surely you threw in a few hundred dollars too, when I bought stocks, didn't you?"

Sternli had not even thought of such a thing, and according to his strict code it would have been dishonest.

Only once had Sternli seen Donovan weak and uncontrolled. The day Katherine died. She escaped Donovan's domination by quietly slipping out of his hands. By dying she had deprived him of the final victory of subduing her. To hold her he had forced her to give birth to one child after another. Only the first and the last had lived, Howard and Chloe.

When Katherine died, Donovan made Sternli stay in the room with him constantly. Sternli watched the big man walking up and down for nights, mumbling to himself.

To have seen Donovan in an hour of weakness was a sentence of destruction, as if a slave had known where a king's treasure was hidden. Opposite me sat a man of fifty who looked seventy, half blind, helpless, penniless.

"I don't know why Mr. Donovan sent me the five hundred dollars, Dr. Cory. Exactly the sum he loaned me and then collected again! Five hundred dollars. Did he choose just that sum with some purpose? Did he want me to believe he regretted many things he had unconsciously done to hurt me? I am sure he always meant to be kind. He did not die without remembering me! It is not the money, it is the thought that makes me happy."

"He did not know he was going to die," I said.

"Oh yes," Sternli replied quietly. "He had known for more than a year that his days were numbered."

The revelation shocked me. It suddenly put Donovan in

another light. It gave me a perspective on his character I had not had before.

"How could he have known about the accident in advance?" I asked, surprised.

"Oh, he did not," Sternli answered with a wan smile, "but he knew he was ill. There was no hope. The doctors gave him only one more year."

"Nephritic," I diagnosed, remembering the color of Donovan's face, whitish, with a yellow tinge. He had suffered from nephritic degeneration of the kidneys, which is usually associated with a similar process in the liver.

"Yes," Sternli nodded. "That is what they told him. W. H. used to drink alone. Solitary drinkers are dangerous. I sometimes thought he chose to get drunk, not because he liked it, but because he wanted to blank out his thoughts. He was tired from considering so many new and powerful projects. He was hounded by his own intelligence. Often he called for me in the middle of the night and dictated for hours. I gave him a dictaphone once for his birthday, but he still kept sending for me at the most ungodly hours. Then during the last years he started to drink in secret. He did not like anybody to see and he never invited me to share a bottle with him. I think he hated alcohol, really."

Sternli suddenly fell into contemplation, forgetting me.

So Donovan had been trying to escape himself. Did he have a conscience, then? And what was he trying to forget?

"He had coaxed the truth out of his physicians. Nobody could lie to Donovan. When he learned his days were numbered, he changed," Sternli said.

"Became kinder, I suppose," I prompted to help him on, but Sternli shook his head.

He polished his glasses again and smiled. His myopic eyes were wide open.

"No. Not what is generally understood by the word *kindness*. The first thing he did was to fire me, without a pension. He gave up his chairmanship to his son. He turned over to his family everything but the houses and apartments where he used to live. He had a score of mansions all over the country, and an apartment in every town. In each of his personal dwellings breakfast was brought in every morning whether the master was there or the bed empty. The servants had to knock, to enter, to take away the tray after a reasonable length of time. The same at luncheon. In each house each night full dinner for eight was served at the same time. Donovan loved to pay surprise visits, arriving just as the first course was served. He had found this custom described in a book about Spain in the reign of Philip II, and it appealed to his sense of seigniory. 'I am omnipresent,' he used to say, 'and if I pay I expect service!' But when they told him he was going to die, he closed all the houses. He had a plan for the limited time he had left."

"What plan?" I asked. I felt I was close to Donovan's secret now.

"He said he wanted to balance his books," Sternli answered. His eyes behind the sharp glass were wondering. "I do not know what he meant by that."

Suddenly Sternli became restless and looked at his watch.

"I must not talk any longer," he said, as if only now he was aware he had been telling me a story he had never related to anyone before. He felt so greatly embarrassed he had to apologize.

"Forgive an old man for talking too much."

He was in a hurry to leave, but I asked him not to go. I suddenly received the brain's commands more strongly than ever before. As if the brain had been listening all the time and was going to take its part in the conversation now.

"Since you are unattached," I said, prompted by the brain, "would you mind working for me? I can pay you as much as Donovan did."

"Work for you?" Sternli's face flushed in happy surprise. "But how could I be of service to you?"

"I want you to open an account at the Merchants Bank on Hollywood Boulevard. You will find a roll of bills in my overcoat pocket. Please deposit them," I said.

Sternli looked myopically toward the closet, and while he was opening the door, I took the checkbook from my wallet and wrote: "To the order of Mr. Anton Sternli, $100,000, Roger Hinds."

Sternli returned with the money in his hands.

"How much shall I take?" he asked.

"All of it. Don't count it. Just pay it in. And take this with you."

I handed him the check.

The brain's orders suddenly stopped. I felt pain creeping on me and grabbed the hypodermic which Janice had prepared for a return of the attack.

Sternli took the key and the check. He held the paper close to his eyes, stared at it open-mouthed. He had recognized Donovan's handwriting.

DECEMBER 2

TODAY I got up for the first time. I shall have to wear this plaster cast for weeks to come. My back still hurts and when I move I feel like a turtle.

I can't stay in bed any longer. Donovan is ordering me to get up, and my body aches with his commands.

Janice has to dress me; I cannot bend over. She has brought me enormously big shirts and a suit large enough for a Barnum giant, to fit over the cumbersome cast.

The brain has gained strength enormously. Its commands enter my mind as clearly as if I heard it speak, loud-voiced and determined, close to my ear.

If only I could inform it that I am out of the running. I ordered Schratt to convey that information to the brain in Morse, but I am not sure he knows Morse well enough to tap out a clear message.

I want to go back to the desert. I want to watch the brain's development myself. But it orders me to stay here.

It has told me to get in touch with the murderer, Cyril Hinds, whose trial comes up soon.

DECEMBER 3

STERNLI has opened the account in his own name and brought back a power of attorney for me. Now I can sign checks and won't have to wait for Donovan's signature. I asked Sternli how it feels to earn fifty dollars a week and be able to write a check for thousands.

He seemed to be shocked at my harmless joke, and stared at me aghast through his thick glasses. He stammered a few words, and I had to put him at ease again. He often watches me doubtfully since I "forged" Donovan's handwriting so cleverly.

When Janice came in, Sternli's blue eyes lighted up, and he forgot I was in the room. He adores her. I don't know what Janice does to make all these men idolize her.

She is unselfish. Whatever she does, she never considers herself. That may be her simple secret.

DECEMBER 4

THE brain paralyzes me at certain times. Formerly when it gave its orders I willingly followed the command. At first I was even obliged to concentrate to follow what it wanted. Otherwise my own personality interfered with the response. Now I cannot resist.

I have tried. I have fought. In vain.

Today it told me to pick up a pen and write. Janice was in the room and I did not want her to see me acting like a hypnotist's subject.

She had just brought in my dinner and we were talking about Sternli and his strange adoration for her, which she defended smilingly, when the brain cut in. I felt my tongue tighten. I was forced to get up and go over to the writing desk. I watched my performance as detached as a stranger standing yards away from me. I wanted to stop. But I still moved mechanically.

Janice had never before witnessed a manifestation of Donovan's will, and she was frightened. She was level-headed enough, however, not to call the floor physician.

I sat down at the desk and began to write. Janice spoke to me, astonished at first, then quickly alarmed when I did not answer.

There was nothing unusual in my attitude except the expression on my face. During this period of telepathic communication my eyes stare, my face loses all expression and looks blank as if it were made of wax.

Janice knew me well enough to be sure immediately that something like a hypnotic trance was holding me.

I wrote on the paper: "Cyril Hinds, Nat Fuller."

Cyril Hinds was the murderer. Nat Fuller's name appeared for the first time.

The spell ended as quickly as it had come and I gained control over my movements again.

Janice's face was chalk. Her eyes held depthless horror. "You were writing with your left hand," she stammered. "The brain . . ."

I went back to the table and began to eat, trying to act as calmly as I could, shaken to find that for the first time I had been unable to resist the brain's command.

"What of it?" I asked. "You know the brain is alive. It communicates with me from time to time. This step forward in my experiment will make history. Since the human brain never reaches full development during the life of the human body, I may be able to let the brain ripen by keeping it artificially alive. This telepathic contact is only the beginning. Have you never heard that the man who experiments must be willing to take any personal risk? The world has to thank many scientists who became their own guinea pigs to achieve great discoveries."

"But it is controlling you—not you controlling it!" She was upset.

"You are mistaken," I answered, wanting to break off the discussion I had foreseen and dreaded. If only she had been a hired assistant, she would not have dared to challenge me. But she was my wife.

"I am submitting to the brain's control deliberately, and I can stop any time I choose."

Janice looked at me, pale, her big eyes dark. She read my thoughts and knew I was not telling the truth.

"Donovan is dead!" she said.

"Dead?" I said slowly. "A doctor's definition of death is different from a layman's. Even when a man is legally declared dead his brain may continue to send out electric waves. Sometimes a man is already dead for the physician while he is still breathing. Where does life begin and where does it end? In the eyes of the world Donovan is dead, but his brain lives on. Does that mean Donovan is still alive?"

"No," she said, "but he lives through you. He forces you to act for him!"

"That is a contradiction," I said. "That will not stand up under analysis."

Janice looked at me. Her face seemed to have shrunk and it was transparent as Chinese silk. She had worried about me for years, and the conviction that I had lost myself in this experiment now broke through her self-control. I knew she wanted to avoid any serious discussion on any subject, but her concern was stronger than her resolution.

"Donovan is dead and cremated," she said. "What you call his living brain is a scientific freak, a dangerous morbid creation you have nursed in a test tube."

"Donovan is still alive and kicking," I answered. "He even has written messages."

"You derive your conviction from science," she stated. "Mine is from faith."

"Listen to Schratt's disciple," I gibed. "You are afraid! Fear threatens the integrity of the personality, but it is good for you and others to have some anxiety, some dread of consequences, some degree of self-consciousness. These restrain your dealings with others. But don't judge my task by common codes of living. I go beyond them."

"How far?" she asked.

"Until I understand the functioning of this brain, its will, its desires, its motives," I said. "I am gathering facts. If I knew the relative position of all the phenomena which comprise Donovan's brain, I could draw a parallel to our ordinary process of thinking and clear up many questions which are unanswerable now. I am penetrating more deeply into human consciousness than any man has done before."

Janice did not reply.

I hated her at that moment. I hated her aloof, detached expression of listening to a voice I could not hear. She was guided not by her intelligence, but by her intuition. She had knowledge not gained through her senses which came from another plane that cannot be explored scientifically.

My intellectual power is based on precise reasoning. I could not deal with Janice. I was at a disadvantage.

We sat silent opposite each other.

"It has too much power over you. You cannot resist it any longer," Janice said finally.

"Any moment I choose I can stop the experiment!"

I was defending myself and I hated her for it.

"You can't. I just saw what is happening myself!"

I got up, walked over to the desk, and picked up the message Donovan had dictated to me.

"I wish you would leave me alone. There is no use arguing with you. I did not ask you to interfere with my work. You are disturbing me. Don't you see?"

It was plainly put. I had to hurt her to make her leave me.

She turned without looking back and left the room.

I am well enough to live alone in a hotel where I shall not be interfered with.

DECEMBER 4

THE futile discussion with Janice upset me, and the tiring repetition of the lines: "Amidst the mists . . ." kept me awake half the night. When I got up I was shaky.

Is Donovan's brain going insane? That monomaniacal endless returning of the same phrase indicates a decrease in intrapsychic co-ordination, an impediment of the logical combination of thoughts.

This stereotypic repetition of phonetic expressions is alarming. The sick mind imagines it hears the same monotonous sound, the same melody repeating endlessly. It considers the same situation, reproduces the same mental picture, repeats the same lines until their meaning acquires a symbolism culminating in a supernatural message, the expression of providence, which the unhealthy imagination readily accepts and interprets according to its own wish dream.

If Donovan's brain becomes measurably insane and can still influence me against my resistance, this case will become difficult to handle. Since it already has such power over my will that sometimes I am helpless, I must think of an emergency brake to paralyze the brain at the extreme moment. I must find a solution, and soon!

TODAY I went back to the Roosevelt Hotel. I feel strong enough but still must wear the plaster cast. It inconveniences me less than before.

The human body can adjust itself to most unnatural conditions.

NATHANIEL FULLER.

The name has repeated itself in Donovan's messages. Two Nathaniel Fullers are listed in the telephone directory. One at a gas station at Olympic Boulevard, the other a lawyer in the Subway Terminal Building, on Hill Street.

I was sure the brain means the lawyer.

I rang the office of Fuller, Hogan and Dunbar, and asked for an appointment. Fuller's secretary inquired my business, but I could not tell her what I wanted for I did not know myself.

"Who recommended you to Mr. Fuller?" she asked.

I mentioned W. H. Donovan's name and immediately she became very polite. A few seconds later I had Fuller on the phone.

He asked me to come in any time during the afternoon and did not ask questions. He seems a good lawyer.

It was one of the warm pleasant Indian-summer days. I took a taxi downtown. For the first time in years I felt relaxed and happy. The tension which had gripped me so long, never letting me breathe freely, driving me on and on even when I slept, had suddenly left me.

I played with the fancy of going away soon. I wanted a rest. Perhaps to New Orleans for Christmas. Perhaps take Janice with me. In strange alarm I analyzed my thoughts. I was suddenly including Janice in my future life, forgetting our misunderstandings and tensions. Was I unconsciously trying to run away from Donovan? Had I become afraid of the experiment? I must watch myself carefully and not let the subconscious interfere with my activities.

I announced my name to the girl behind Fuller's reception desk. She picked up the phone in a hurry and a few seconds later Fuller came out. He was small and stocky, dressed by an expensive tailor, and his gray hair carefully groomed.

Packed as I was in the cast, I presented a strange appearance, but he registered no astonishment and took me straight into a room with a sign on the door: "Library. Quiet, Please."

The silence which suddenly engulfed us was abnormal, as if the walls were specially sound-proofed. Though it was early afternoon, the Venetian blinds were drawn and neon tubes threw a diffuse light through the room and left our features shadowless. It was a good light in which Fuller could easily observe the expression in his clients' faces.

He asked me to sit down and took a chair opposite me at the long, glass-topped conference table.

"W. H. sent you," he said in a pleasant, unaggressive voice, and looked at me with an air of friendly lassitude.

"Yes. He mentioned your name before he died."

"What did he tell you?" Fuller murmured.

"You have been one of his lawyers, I understand," I said. "And he told me I could talk to you frankly, if I ever needed legal advice."

"You need it now?" he asked, and looked squarely at me. "What can I do for you?"

"I want you to take over the Hinds murder case," I said.

He leaned back in his chair, which he slowly rocked on its slender legs.

"Hinds is guilty of first-degree murder and this is one of the most cruel cases I have heard during my twenty years as a criminal lawyer!" He looked down at the table and spoke slowly as if to gain time.

The soundless room may have hidden microphones. The neon lights may be there for making secret pictures.

A few dictaphones were standing about, and a voice-recording machine. Perhaps every word I spoke was preserved on wax as evidence against me.

"I am prepared to pay you a bonus of fifty thousand dollars, besides your ordinary fee, if you can exonerate Hinds," I said.

He sat silent and pondered a moment. He did not take my offer seriously and was trying to decide how he could get rid of me without offending me. The amount was preposterous, out of all proportion, even for this case.

In my cheap, ill-fitting suit, I did not give the impression of being a man who could pay a lawyer fifty thousand dollars.

I looked on the glass-covered table and our eyes met as in a mirror. It seemed a trick of his, watching people in the glass top. It annoyed me.

"Exonerate. You mean acquittal by the jury?" he asked to gain time. He was reaching for the bell.

I took a wad of money from my pocket and laid it in front of him.

He pulled back his hand from the bell.

Uneasy, he tried to get me into a discussion to find out more about me.

"Will you please tell me your motive in this, Dr. Cory?" he said.

"Just assume I am fighting capital punishment," I answered.

He nodded. This was a basis for discussion. Many people in the world will support their convictions with good cash.

"I understand. You want Hinds spared, as an example. We might be able to save him from hanging, and later get him released."

"You misunderstand me," I said. "I want Hinds acquitted. Pronounced innocent by the jury."

"You contradict your first assertion that you only want to save his life," Fuller answered uneasily. He could not be sure what I was after.

"I am not here to argue with you," I answered, knowing the brain wanted Hinds to be free at once.

"But there is no doubt of this man's guilt!" Fuller exclaimed. "And I never touch hopeless cases."

I got up, ready to leave.

Fuller said hastily: "You must give me a few days to

study the case. I hope there will be a way. But if I can't see it, I cannot take the case."

"I am sure you will take it," I said.

He went with me to the door.

"Would you object to depositing the amount of the fee until the trial is over?" he asked.

"Of course not," I said. "Ring me at the Roosevelt Hotel tomorrow morning and you can have the check."

I stopped in the reception room.

"Could you get permission for me to talk to Hinds?" I asked.

"Of course. I assume he is related to you?" Fuller asked politely.

"No," I answered.

Fuller hid his surprise.

"He must be a good friend of yours!"

"To tell the truth," I said, "I have never seen Hinds in my life, and only came across his name a few days ago."

This time Fuller was dumbfounded.

DECEMBER 8

TODAY Sternli left for Reno to see Miss Geraldine Hinds. I told Sternli that Donovan, dying, had told me to look after this woman and also to get in touch with another Hinds, a plumber in Seattle.

Sternli becomes more and more bewildered. He cannot comprehend how sometimes my writing is Donovan's, how I draw money from an account that is not mine. And how can this illogical curiosity about people I do not seem to know be explained?

Sternli is glad to get away from me.

DECEMBER 9

FULLER telephoned me this morning. He has spoken to the chief jailer at the county prison to get permission for me to see Cyril Hinds.

98

As Fuller could not explain my relation to the accused, that official wants to talk to me before he gives consent.

Fuller has studied the case and in his opinion only one defense could succeed. He would not discuss his plan over the phone. He told me he would see me at my hotel.

Fuller's optimism sounded forced. I have a strong conviction that without the money I have promised him he would never touch this case. Before he hung up he reminded me to deposit the fee in his bank.

I am sure the brain is thinking clearly. It cannot be insane as I feared, for its instructions are precise and seem logical. The one disturbing element is that repetitious line, which enters my mind mostly when I am asleep. It sometimes also crops up during the day, without warning, and I always am unable to suppress the incongruous feeling of terror that accompanies it.

The brain's identification with my consciousness has increased, and by having penetrated to another part of my cerebellum it may already be transmitting my sensory impressions to its own consciousness. It may receive the sensations of sound and sight and feel the gusto reactions of my palate. I cannot prove that yet, but I believe the brain lives through me the full life of a normal human being.

If my theory is right, Donovan's brain should be able to converse with other people, since my hearing relayed to its nervous centers, and my tongue directed by its commands, are all the tools it needs for intelligent self-expression.

The brain uses my motor nerves like instruments controlled by a deep-sea diver, working in a diving belt. Donovan may see the world, through my eyes, and he should be able to see me too, when I look at myself in the mirror.

DECEMBER 10

On my way to the Hall of Justice I stopped at a tobacco store and bought a dozen Upman cigars.

I have not smoked a cigar in years. I dislike the cold wet taste. I made the purchase under command.

At once I lit one of the cigars, but I had no sensation of

taste. When I tried to throw the rag away, however, my hand held it fast, and I had to continue to puff slowly, as if enjoying the smoke profoundly.

I was smoking with my left hand, which is unusual, as I smoke cigarettes with my right hand.

Donovan was left-handed!

If I could find out what cigars Donovan smoked, I would have part of the proof I need. Have I lost my sense of taste? Last night, with a sudden dislike for meat, I ordered nothing but vegetables for dinner. They had no taste at all. Was Donovan a vegetarian? I must inquire. Sternli would know.

I inhaled the cigar smoke deeply, and it was like breathing tasteless water vapor. Does Donovan's brain receive these impressions instead of my five senses? Or has this state of schizophrenia deadened my physical sensibilities because the brain, ruling my hippocampal gyrus, has taken over the sensations of smell and taste?

The brain's penetration is slow, but irresistibly it has engulfed every part of my cerebellum.

One day it may take over my activities completely. The impulses which prompt my actions will generate in Washington Junction, while my body roams the world directed by remote control.

Thus in a future state a human being could be commanded by a chosen super-brain and be guided robot-like from a central station.

The county jail covers six upper floors of the Hall of Justice, a huge square building at Broadway and Temple.

I entered a room with the inscription: "Public Relations," and an employee in shirt sleeves took me nine floors up to the office of the chief jailer.

The colored elevator boy wore the smart gray outfit of the sheriff's office, with the six-pointed star of the police force.

At the ninth floor an inner door with thick iron bars protected the entrance to the jail. A guard opened this side to scrutinize the passengers in the elevator.

My shirt-sleeved attendant must have seen curiosity in my eyes, for he began to spiel like a tourist's guide, informing me that more than two thousand prisoners were here—

the largest county jail in the world. Eighteen hundred men and two hundred women, he said proudly.

At the ninth floor we stepped out and crossed a corridor to the private office of the chief jailer. We passed through an anteroom, the walls of which were plastered with photographs of the sheriff's farm, where prisoners work out the greater part of their sentences.

The chief was a man of about fifty, dressed smartly in a gray-green uniform. He seemed to be expecting me. The man in shirt sleeves left, and the chief waited till the door had closed behind him.

He stood up then and walked over to a second writing-desk, which looked unused. It was of heavy black wood, elaborately carved, and there to impress visitors. A blue vase with one dahlia in it stood on the blotter. On the wall behind hung a huge electric clock with a jeweler's name printed on the dial, a present for services rendered. Photographs of officers and their wives adorned the walls. It was a room where a man has spent most of his life.

The chief sat down ponderously in a high-backed chair.

"Mr. Fuller phoned me," he said. "He asked me to let you talk to Hinds."

He looked reflectively through his spectacles. He gave the impression of being a scholarly man who did not belong in a uniform.

"Yes. I asked Mr. Fuller to talk to you," I answered.

"Mr. Fuller is the most successful—and also the most expensive—criminal lawyer in this state," the chief began again. "I wonder what prompted him to take over a hopeless case."

"Has Hinds confessed?" I asked.

"Oh no—his kind never confess," the chief said quietly. "But Hinds has no money himself. As I understand it, you are greatly interested in the case. Have you engaged Mr. Fuller's services for Hinds?"

He smiled at me benevolently, and I felt certain our conversation was being recorded somewhere in the next room.

"I am a pathologist," I answered, "and extremely interested in cases like Hinds's. Is there any objection to my talking to him?"

The chief pondered. He was slightly disappointed, for he had expected an answer to his question. But since Fuller had not chosen to inform him, I had no reason to tell more than my lawyer.

"I know you are not related to Hinds," the chief said. He had made investigations.

We sat silent for a moment until he began again.

"Hinds is much disliked in this prison. He gives us a great deal of trouble, and I have had to put him in solitary confinement for a couple of days, for striking an officer. That isn't done in my prison. The officers are courteous and friendly. The other prisoners solidly dislike Hinds."

The chief looked up and smiled a little with the air of a professor pleased with his class.

"My boys despise cowardice. They don't mind cruelty. They even look up to a mass murderer. But this cowardly way of killing!"

He was ready to give a lecture on criminal psychology. Jailers, like physicians, are overcharged with case histories and have to have an outlet. I have rarely met a doctor who did not write. Jailers are as bad.

I had to listen politely, for it was in his power to refuse me admittance to Hinds.

"You know him well?" he asked casually.

"No," I replied, glad he had not asked if I knew Hinds at all.

"Well, he does not know you either." The chief smiled. "That makes your request unusual."

"I am writing a book about psychopathology," I answered, to give him a motive he could accept.

He nodded.

"You know the charges?" he asked. When I did not reply, he explained: "He ran over a woman with his car—purposely!"

He studied my blank face and added: "The cruelest part of it is he backed up and ran over her again in reverse, crushing her face. Then he drove away. But we got him. The car left plain tire marks."

"His sweetheart?" I asked.

"His mother," the chief said.

As if that revelation was too brutal for him, even accustomed as he was to cruel slayings, he contined: "Of course Hinds does not remember having hit anybody. He said he was coming from a party and was slightly drunk. A strange coincidence he just happened to kill his mother!"

"The motive?" I asked again.

The chief shrugged, suddenly drying up. As keeper of a strange assortment of prisoners, he was supposed to be impartial, but he seemed to have a strong personal dislike for Hinds.

After a certain length of time the atmosphere of a prison affects keepers and inmates alike. Guards, after a few years of duty, begin to see the world differently. Right and wrong acquire only abstract meanings, and a strong understanding for the motive of crimes develops.

Only a man who has worked with his hands can understand workmen. Only one who has sailed ships knows men who love the sea. Every future judge ought to have an apprenticeship as guard in a prison. Justice should not be taught theoretically, alone.

But in the Hinds case prisoners and warden alike had condemned the murderer.

"May I see Hinds?" I asked.

The chief got up and rang a bell.

"I had to segregate him or the other prisoners would have killed him. I have never seen such antagonism among them. They would poison his food if they had the chance."

An officer entered and saluted leisurely.

"Take Dr. Cory to the fifteenth floor," the chief said, "and get Hinds."

The man saluted again and we left.

We walked over to the elevator, and the iron barred door slid back.

"Fifteen," the officer said to the colored elevator boy. He looked at me out of the corner of his eye as if he resented my going to see Hinds.

We arrived. The door opened into a large room where tables with ten-inch partitions down the middle separated visitors from the prisoners.

"Wait here. I have to get him from Highpower," the officer said gruffly.

Highpower is the tenth floor, where they keep the murderers.

I sat down on the bench and read the sign on the partition: "This side for Attorneys."

Another side read: "Prisoners."

The room was rather crowded. Prisoners in blue jeans entered, sat down, and talked in low voices. The attorneys did not take off their hats, and everyone seemed to be in a hurry.

The place hummed with voices. Faces were pale in the yellow light.

My policeman returned and Hinds was with him.

At the iron-barred door, guarded by two officers, Hinds was set free. The one who had accompanied him pointed sullenly at me, then turned at once as if he was afraid of being infected by proximity to Hinds.

Hinds stepped searchingly forward. He did not look in any direction but mine, but he must have felt the antagonism his presence generated everywhere. The voices went on humming, somehow louder, but it was as if everyone had turned his back to Hinds.

He stepped up to me and looked at me blankly.

"My name is Patrick Cory," I said, across the width of table, and stretched out my hand, which Hinds ignored. He sat down opposite me and gazed at me as if I were the prisoner and he the visitor from outside.

He was a good-looking boy, about twenty-five, well built, lean and muscular. His straight blond hair was combed back, his blue eyes clear, but his mouth was hard and nearly lipless. There was not one soft feature in his face. He was the prototype of discontented youth, who, with a strange concept of bravery, do not price life very highly.

This boy might be cynical up to the steps of the hangman's trap. He might joke on his way to the gallows, and act his role right to the death. Or he might suddenly lose this grand, contemptuous manner and fall into a coma of fear, which would change him to a cringing coward in a second's time.

If he had had it in mind to play insane, he might have carried out the scheme until he really was mad and had to be confined in an asylum.

But as it happened he considered himself a hero, and with a conceit stronger than his will to live, he treated the whole world with contempt. He was a fanatic without a cause and there is no use arguing with a fanatic.

"I wanted to ask you if you know a Roger Hinds," I said.

He had expected a different opening. He mistrusted me for he was suspicious of the tricks the law might play to get a confession out of him.

"Well," he answered gruffly, "I had an uncle who hanged himself, if you mean him."

"How long ago?" I inquired.

"Before I was born, but I remember my mother talking about him."

The mention of his mother did not move him.

We sat quiet for a moment. Hinds stared at his hands, which were thin and white, with broad nails.

I was on my own, without any compulsion from the brain, and I could ask whatever my curiosity prompted.

"Then you know Warren Horace Donovan?"

"Not personally," Hinds said. "Isn't he the guy who got killed in a plane a few weeks ago? I read it in the papers!"

He kept on staring at his hands, unmoved by my questions. We maneuvered like two fencers, each waiting for the other to open up.

"I am here to help you as much as I can."

Immediately he was resentful.

"I don't need help. If they want to hang me, okay. But they can't break me down. They're treating me lousy, but I don't care."

He kept up his resistance by hating everybody.

"Mr. Fuller is going to defend you," I said.

"That's what he told me. He's a big shot, they say. I wonder who hired him."

He looked at me questioningly, but the sullen expression returned quickly. He wanted to be on his own. It would only weaken his self-reliance to know someone was helping him. Querulously he reversed cause and effect to put himself in the right.

"They can't do anything to me. I didn't run over the old woman purposely. They can't prove it. Even that big lawyer can't do nothing but tell the truth."

He suddenly grinned.

"They sent you to make me talk. Go on, tell them I didn't run over her purposely!"

In stating his innocence he repeated the same phrases. He had laid out his defense. If he refused to confess, the law was powerless, he thought.

"If you are innocent they will set you free!" I said.

"They've got to. I have a lot of things to do. I'd hate to go now!"

His thin mouth closed hard and the muscles in his jaw sprang out.

"Tell 'em they won't get me down. Even if they put me in the hole again and beat me up, and give me rotten food and turn all the boys here against me! I know their tricks. They can't hurt me! And they're going to pay for it! Just let me out of here!"

He got up. The interview was over so far as he was concerned. Through me he had broadcast to the world his contempt of it.

"Even if they hang me, they won't see me yellow," he said loudly, and walked back to the officer, his head up, knowing the room looked after him.

The elevator took me down.

This boy is a murderer if ever there was one.

But he had been badly introduced to live, and no one bothered to develop forces in him which would restrain him. He is not entirely to blame, though there was no reason to defend him either.

He will kill again if he thinks anybody stands in his way.

But what had Donovan to do with this boy? Cyril Hinds is Donovan's illegitimate child, Donovan's action is understandable.

Fuller may know the truth.

DECEMBER 11

THE desk clerk handed me a note inviting me to dine at Howard Donovan's house in Encino, on the 13th at seven o'clock.

I will certainly go to see him and listen to all the questions which I am not willing to answer.

I knew Howard would turn up again!

Schratt phoned. He told me Janice is back in Washington Junction. When I inquired why she had gone home, he joked that Janice and he were good friends and they were just taking advantage of my absence to see each other alone.

The brain is doing fine, he says. Size and electric output still increasing.

While Schratt waited at the phone for instructions, my subconscious fear suddenly found expression. I ordered him to keep the brain at its present weight and strength, not to feed it too much. My mouth was suddenly so dry my voice sounded harsh.

"I understand," Schratt replied elusively.

I hung up quickly, angry with myself. Had I admitted I was becoming afraid? My order could not be explained otherwise, and Schratt would interpret it so.

Fear is a natural reaction of all organisms which have weapons of self-defense. I belong to this class, and I have no reason to blame myself. Fear is innate.

I was suddenly tired. Instead of phoning Fuller to tell him about my visit to the jail, I lay down to rest.

I took a sleeping draught. I did not want to receive Donovan's messages.

DECEMBER 12

At ten this morning the phone rang and, still under the influence of the drug, I answered. I had a good night's rest. Even the strange line: "Amidst the mists . . ." which had accompanied my sleep for weeks, had not troubled me.

A Mr. Pulse was calling from the lobby. Fuller had told him to see me. He thought it would be more convenient to talk in my room. Could he come up?

I asked him to wait, had the barber sent up, and indulged in the luxury of being shaved. Then I dressed, and examined myself in the mirror, relaxed for the first time in months.

Suddenly my reflection became a transparent opacity; the sensation lasted only for a moment, but then Donovan's brain took possession of me more strongly than ever.

I stared into the mirror, scrutinizing myself from head to foot as if I had never seen my reflection before. I breathed deep, moved my shoulders, without being actually aware of my body. I pinched my wrist with my fingers, but though the skin reddened I felt no pain.

Not walking like myself at all, but with a slight limp in my right leg, I crossed the room, picked up one of the Upman cigars, and began to smoke it.

As always, I was aware of everything I did, but for the first time I was a prisoner in my own body, with no power to do anything except what I was commanded.

I recalled the stages I had passed through during this experiment with Donovan's brain. At first I had concentrated on Donovan's orders, forcing myself to understand him. During the second phase I easily interpreted commands, and acted accordingly. Finally I had permitted the brain to direct my body.

Until now I was unable to resist. I had lost control completely!

The brain could walk my body in front of a car, throw it out of the window, put a bullet through my head with my own hands. I could only cry out from the despair of my imprisonment, but even the words my mouth formed were those the brain wanted to hear.

A wave of terror engulfed me as I realized I was like a man fastened in a machine which moves his hands and feet against his will.

The frightening sensation passed and I was free again. I felt the smoke of the cigar in my mouth, though I could not taste it. I stopped limping, and the dull pressure in the kidney area ceased, as if I had just recovered from an attack of nephritis and anuria.

When Donovan's brain takes possession of my nervous system, it re-creates the conditions of its own body— the pains in the kidneys, the limp, the same tastes and distastes in food and tobacco. It may soon revert to drink!

Suddenly I remembered the Mr. Pulse waiting for me and phoned the desk clerk to send him up.

A few minutes later a huge man entered, filling the doorway with his bulging presence. Pulse stood over six feet tall. He wore his hair long like a musician's in a Victorian comedy, and his fat face was set in a cushion of double chin. He looked affably at me with his eyes proptosed as one sees quite often in Graves' disease.

Introducing himself, he swayed into the room like a hippopotamus. When he sat down, the chair disappeared under him.

He came straight to the point.

"Hinds will be tried next week," he said. "I have studied the case."

I had to strain to hear him, for with a voice in strange contrast to his bulk, he whispered thinly, as if afraid of being overheard. His hypertrophied thyroid was causing a pressure on the recurrent laryngeal nerve, which gave his voice a high pitch.

He expounded on his findings: "The jurors are influenced mostly by the impression they get of the accused, and less by the actual facts of the case. A man with a charming manner might receive easier punishment for the same crime than somebody else, like Hinds for instance, who does not bother to put on a good show. I am glad we have no women on this jury; they are guided mostly by their sympathies."

Not a muscle of his fat face changed, but he moved his hands to make up for his lack of animation.

Pulse seemed to have studied the case thoroughly, and he quickly sketched a plan to save Hinds. Not once did he mention Fuller.

Three hundred names of potential jurors, Pulse explained, were drawn at random from the voting lists and posted on a panel in the court house. Of these three hundred citizens more than two hundred would not care to serve as jurors; they could be discarded at once.

The rest had to be investigated.

Pulse opened his brief-case and took out a list.

"You see," he whispered listlessly. "I used to work for Southern Tramway. We had minutest information about every juror. Too many unjust claims are brought against big companies, accident claims mostly, and if a friend of the plaintiff should be among the jurors, a lot of harm can be done. That's why we kept files on everybody, or"—he smiled and showed small white teeth like a woman's—"nearly everybody!"

"Do you still work for Southern Tramway?" I asked.

"Oh no. It doesn't pay enough, but I have a copy of their files!"

He had already found out how many were unwilling to serve as jurors in the Hinds case. Here were the rest: sixty-seven names.

Among these were twenty-eight retired business men, former petty city officials, pensioned military men, all eager to serve just to make the three dollars a day.

"The prosecuting attorney likes men like these. They know the routine and the defense attorney cannot rattle them. We know all of them! Well, they can be approached!"

Small droplets of sweat dotted Pulse's forehead, and his voice dropped lower.

"But the rest require some serious work! I can find only a few of their names in my files and must send out my men to inquire into the private affairs of these other would-be jurors. Most people have something in their lives—something they want to hide."

His protruding eyes suddenly discovered the cigars on the table, and a flicker of interest crossed his face.

"Please help yourself," I said. Immediately his hand shot out and he grabbed an Upman. For the first time he showed an emotion.

"Upman's!" he exclaimed. "Dollar apiece!" And he went on talking with the same impersonal tone, but his attitude was cordial.

"Here's an example. Last time one of the jurors, a new one to us, was an undertaker, married, about fifty years old. He had a pretty secretary who helped him run his outfit. We found out about his personal interest in the girl. Well, he was shocked when we told him what we knew. He would have hated to have the affair uncovered by the defense. So he accepted twenty-five hundred and we had a 'pill in the box.'"

He inhaled the smoke with relish.

"A 'pill in the box' is a juror who is on the side of the defendant," he explained. "It does not mean the juror has

110

been suborned, but sometimes he is in a quandary himself how to cast his vote and this money helps him decide. It prevents him, too, from condemning an innocent man and being party to legal murder!"

Pulse's big eyes twinkled at me amusedly and he suddenly asked: "Well, in case we have to do something about all twelve jurors, are you prepared to put down that much?"

"I must talk to Mr. Fuller first," I answered.

Pulse pursed his lips.

"The case can only be handled through me, as I am anonymous and your lawyer is a public figure, so to speak. You understand?" He spoke listlessly.

Fuller did not want to be mixed up in bribing jurors; he did not want to know anything about the arrangements.

"My fee will be five thousand dollars, and I cannot vouch for the jury's decision," Pulse added, and hid his face in a cloud of smoke.

I did not care how much money found its way from Donovan's account into the pocket of Pulse's tweed coat, but I wanted for once to produce some show of human emotion in that fat face.

"It's a high price to pay with no guarantee of results!" I said.

Pulse hunched his fat shoulders. "The charge is *first-*degree murder, and the whole case is very delicate to handle. Consider how easy it will be for the district attorney. Cyril Hinds never worked at a job in his life. He hung out in pool halls with a questionable crowd. He owed money to everyone and stole if from his old mother, who scrubbed floors at the Biltmore Hotel. The cruel circumstances of her death! Well, doesn't it sound like blackening the character of the accused with cheap exaggerated effects?"

"And why did he kill his mother?" I asked.

Pulse did not look surprised even at this question. "You should know the case better than I do or I would not be here. Hinds stole money from the old lady. He knew she would turn him over to the police this time. It was a little she had saved to bury her. People do things like that; if they have been poor all their lives they want a fine funeral. Maybe she would have gone to the police. To prevent that, Hinds hung around the hotel until she came out to go home. Then he ran over her. Anyway, that is how the district attorney will build up the case. Hit-and-run, with intent to murder."

Pulse stood up as if shocked by his own story.

"Forty thousand is not too much, considering the case," he murmured.

I took him to the door.

"You want it in cash?" I said.

"Of course," he answered, but stopped suddenly and stared at me. His eyes proptosed from their sockets.

"He's not your son?"

"Do I look as old as that?" I asked, astonished.

An expression of strange consternation crossed Pulse's face.

"For a moment you did."

DECEMBER 13

THIS morning I went to the hospital to have the cast removed.

Some actors, to play their roles more smoothly, fasten weights to their hands and feet during the daytime. When they take the weights off for the performance, they experience that same floating, featherlike sensation I had when the nurse cut off the twenty pounds of plaster.

I took a bath, the first time in weeks, and felt boundlessly happy. I discarded the oversized suit and put on one of my old ones.

My back, stiff at first, slowly regained some freedom of motion.

In the pocket of my suit I found the key Sternli had given me. I went to the California Merchants Bank. The sallow-faced teller with the small mustache saw me come in and disappeared at once, to return with the manager.

This man had resigned himself to my being the unorthodox customer I was, and on my request he led me straight to the safe-deposit vault.

After I had turned the combination to the number 114474, the box opened with the key.

It was empty except for a small envelope, which I put in my pocket.

In the street I opened it.

It was a receipt for eighteen hundred and thirty-three dollars and eighteen cents, written in Donovan's handwriting and signed by Roger Hinds. The date was February 7, 1901. The place, San Juan, California.

I turned the paper over, but it gave me no clue why Donovan had kept it so carefully.

San Juan, a small town of about five thousand inhabitants, is the place where Donovan opened his mail-order business.

I put the paper in my wallet. Sternli might tell me more when he returned. I had a wire this morning saying he has contacted Geraldine Hinds.

Donovan's chauffeur was waiting for me in the hotel lobby. Acting on inspiration, or a telepathic contact, I greeted him by his first name: "Hello, Lonza!"

He looked at me dumbfounded; he had never seen me before. Then he grinned all over his face as if I had cracked a joke.

We drove north on Ventura Boulevard toward Encino. I leaned back comfortably, smoking a cigar I did not enjoy.

The borderline between my consciousness and Donovan's became blurred. I talked, but it was Donovan who made me talk. When I walked, this was still my own doing. Or did I only think it was? I had to concentrate hard to know if Donovan moved my hands or I did. But always my thoughts were clear.

At Encino we drove through a big wrought-iron gate, which seemed familiar to me.

We crossed a wide park with dry artificial lakes and empty aviaries. The garden looked forlorn, as if at the owner's death the flowers had stopped blooming.

The car drove up to a sprawling Spanish building, with extensive patios and shady loggias. Most of the windows were shuttered or the blinds drawn.

In the big hall the furniture was hidden under dust covers. A lonely lamp burned in a niche. The house looked as deserted as the gardens.

The chauffeur led me into the library, where a huge log

fire was burning, throwing lambent shadows over the paneled walls. Howard Donovan and his sister waited for me, but to my surprise Fuller, the lawyer, was with them.

"Hello, Cory." Howard walked briskly up to me, his hand outstretched, but stopped with a questioning look on his face. He stared at my hand.

"Sorry," I said, and threw the cigar into the fire. "I forgot. I should have left it outside."

"It's an Upman, isn't it?" Howard said. "My father used to smoke that kind. Funny how a smell will stick in your nose!"

He took my arm amiably.

Fuller only nodded when I greeted him, withdrew to the farthest corner of the room, and busied himself looking at books. Mrs. Chloe Barton spoke my name, but made no move to give me her hand.

Howard walked over to the bar. "A drink, doctor?"

"Thank you, no!" I said.

"Only when nobody's looking," he laughed dryly, obviously thinking of his father. He spoke like a district attorney who wanted to wheedle the witness into good humor for the questioning.

Chloe sat in a corner, watching me. She seemed amused, but in a tense, neurotic way. She was strangely still and the expression in her dark eyes disconcerted me. She watched me with intense interest, drinking in every word of mine. That intensity irritated me. She seemed a woman about ready for a fit of hysterics.

I was surprised how her face had changed. The flesh seemed to have fallen away, and the skin was tightly drawn over the bones. She kept smiling at me, but she had the appearance rather of making a grimace.

We exchanged a few superficial remarks, which did not relieve the tension between us.

"Fuller! A whiskey?" Howard shouted across the room, and his question seemed designed to conceal his thoughts.

"Thank you, I've not finished this one," Fuller mumbled, and went on turning pages.

Howard sat down beside me and jovially slapped my knee. "How is old man Sternli?" he asked.

It was the opening shot of the attack. Fuller closed his

book with a dull slap, put it back on the shelf and turned toward us, while Chloe lifted her folded hands to her cheek in an unnatural gesture. The hands were extremely thin, showing the bones through transparent skin.

"Sternli? He is all right," I said indifferently.

"He is a good man with a remarkable memory. I'd have given him a job if he weren't so nearly blind!" Howard hurried to explain.

"I had an ophthalmologist examine his eyes for lenses."

I did not mean to rebuke my host, but my reply must have sounded like it, for his face reddened. He did not expect to be reprimanded.

It was as if the brain were amusing itself while I looked on, remote and emotionless. I knew every question and answer beforehand, like listening to a well-known story, where every complication is the more enjoyed for being anticipated.

Howard went on talking, but it was evident what he was leading up to.

"So my father told you about Sternli before he died," he said.

Fuller, at the window, made a gesture of impatience. He was irritated at Howard's clumsy approach.

"Oh no, I told you before, your father did not talk. I read about his faithful secretary in the papers." I took another cigar from my pocket and glanced at Fuller. My answer belied the story I had told him about Donovan's advising me to see him, but the lawyer made no move to contradict me.

Howard became impatient. He was not accustomed to making haste slowly. His face contorted and he said sharply: "Let's drop that pretense, Cory. Aren't you getting tired of it?"

He got up and stepped back irritated. The smell of the Upman cigar exaggerated his growing dislike for me.

"Please be more implicit," I helped him along.

Fuller suddenly took over, stepping closer to me.

"Mr. Donovan has made inquiries about you, Dr. Cory. We can stop fencing."

"No doubt he has had detectives on my trail. That's part of the family tradition!" I said smilingly.

"I am an old friend of this family," Fuller replied, on his guard. "When you told me Mr. Donovan senior had sent you to me—and Howard informed me his father had died without leaving a will, and without having talked to anyone at the hour of his death—well, it was my duty to inform Howard and his sister of these contradictions in your story."

He was already sure of my fifty thousand dollars. By telling Howard about me, he might bring more money his way. He was like Yocum, always out for more. But while Yocum was torn by a conscience, Fuller had no such handicap.

"You, as a lawyer, are obligated to secrecy in the affairs of your clients, and I am one of them," I said.

"I know my duty very well, Dr. Cory," Fuller answered, with a sly undertone.

"Then why have you forgotten it?" I asked.

"Why did you spend money on that murderer?" Howard Donovan accused in a theatrical voice. He stood behind me and I had to turn in my chair to face him.

"What murderer?"

"This Cyril Hinds, or whoever he is!"

Howard's face was as grave as a judge's.

"You don't know why?" I was surprised.

"No—but you are using my father's money!" he pointed a fat accusing finger at me. I had to laugh.

Howard was speechless. He looked to Fuller for help.

"Please, let me do the talking for a minute," the lawyer said with elaborate caution. "You are thirty-eight years old, Dr. Cory. You studied medicine at Harvard. When you were twenty-nine you married a girl of small independent means. For a few years you practiced in Los Angeles, but you never earned great sums of money. Then you retired to Washington Junction to carry out some experiments, living on the money you had saved, and afterwards on your wife's."

"Right," I said. "That is my life story."

Fuller went on patiently. "Suddenly you are in possession of seemingly limitless funds. . . . You gave up your experiments and moved back to Los Angeles, interesting yourself in people you had never seen before, like Hinds and

Sternli. . . ." He was dryly adding up the facts as if they were crimes committed.

I interrupted. "How does this concern you, or Mr. Howard Donovan?"

Howard could not keep silent. "Remember our conversation in Phoenix? You denied that my father had talked to you and he told you where he hid his money!"

I stared at him coldly and the silent duel broke his control. His face grew livid and he shouted: "It's my money and you stole it!"

"This is a peculiar accusation, and you will have to prove it," I answered, amused, but in the back of my mind I was afraid.

"Where did you get the money you are throwing around?" Howard cried.

I got up and walked over to the writing-desk, limping. I felt the dull pressure in my kidneys as I sat down heavily.

"Perhaps Mr. Fuller can conjure up some legal reason why I should answer!"

Fuller's voice was smooth and unaggressive. "We can settle this amicably, Dr. Cory. Mr. Donovan is prepared to give you ten per cent of the sum his father left in your trust at the moment of his death. Furthermore the money you have spent or disposed of up to now will not be questioned."

"Any amount?" I asked, looking straight into Fuller's eyes.

He knew I meant the fifty thousand dollars I had put aside for him, but he did not flicker an eyelash.

"Of course," he replied in a friendly tone.

"All right. Will you put that in writing?" I went on.

I saw Howard's eager expression, Fuller's sphinxlike smile. Chloe's face shone white in the half-dark like a grinning death's head.

"Just sign this first." Fuller took a paper from his pocket and put it down in front of me. It was a statement that I had used Donovan's money. I did not bother to read through the paragraphs.

My left hand took the pen and I wrote: "Money received for stamp collection. W. H. Donovan." The pen encircled the name with an oval.

Howard stepped close to pick up the paper. He glanced

at the sentence and signature, with eyes that started from their sockets. Struck dumb, he moved his colorless lips. His fingers, limp, dropped the paper on the floor.

Fuller had watched him closely. "What is it?" he asked, alarmed, and bent down to pick up the paper. But Chloe, having noiselessly left her chair, put her foot on it, stared, and bent down.

Suddenly she clutched her throat and broke into endless hysterical laughter; her face twisted and spots of color sprang out on her white cheeks. She laughed, unable to breathe, until her face, lips, and ears turned cyanotic. The pupils of her eyes dilated widely, failing to react to light-stimuli.

Stepping over to her quickly, I held her arm with my right hand and struck a sharp blow close to her left clavicle. As I saw her eyes grow normal again, I slapped her face twice, hard, holding her up.

The laughter stopped; she could breathe now, but collapsed in my arms as I had expected. I carried her over to the couch and put her down, her face to the wall.

Howard watched me, petrified.

Chloe began to cry, uncontrollably, her body shaking with convulsive sobs.

"Get me a sedative, quickly!" I looked at Howard, who found his own control again at my order.

"There must be something in Chloe's room," he stammered. His aggressiveness had left him; he ran toward the door.

I turned to the patient, who was shaken with retching sobs.

I stayed until Chloe Barton had fallen asleep. Then I told Howard not to move her, to call her physician when she woke.

He listened, staring at me as if I were a ghost. And he is not so far from the truth.

Fuller took me home in his car. He did not talk on our way back; he only said he would see Cyril Hinds, to give him some instructions, but he made no mention of his betrayal.

As soon as I got back to my room, I rang up Schratt. My nerves were rattled. I did not want to crack under the strain. Also that infernal line "Amidst the mists and coldest frosts he thrusts his fists against the posts and still insists he sees the ghosts," was repeating itself again, as if somebody shouted it into my ear.

When I told Shratt to discontinue feeding the brain, he disapproved.

"That's a funny suggestion coming from you, Patrick," he said. "Once you tried to strangle me for meddling with it, and now it's you who are afraid of this experiment!"

"I'm not afraid!" I replied. "I will go on with it, but I need a few days' rest. I'm human too!"

"Are you?" he asked in his slow voice, which infuriated me.

"Stop feeding that brain!" I shouted into the telephone.

After a moment's reflection Schratt answered dryly: "No. I will not interfere with the experiment!"

I was shocked at his obstinacy, which seemed so unreasonable.

"I order you to let the brain fast for the next twenty-four hours!" I said, pronouncing each word slowly to give it weight.

"I cannot accept that order, Patrick. We must go on with it!" And when I shouted at him, he said: "Janice will be back in Los Angeles. You may need her now!"

He hung up.

I sat down, exhausted. What had got into him? How did he dare disobey my orders?

I must get to Washington Junction at once!

But I did not move. My limbs were paralyzed. I lay on my bed for hours, my thoughts spinning until they were a blur of a mass of incoherent pictures. And I fell asleep.

DECEMBER 18

THE telephone rang at seven o'clock. It woke me.

I felt refreshed and in full control of myself. Schratt was right in refusing to obey me. I should not lose my nerve! Now I was grateful for his stubbornness.

Howard Donovan was on the phone. Chloe, he said

refused to let her own doctor see her. She was asking for me. Would I come at once? He was afraid she would have another fit if I did not say yes.

"I have taken the liberty," he concluded, "of sending my car to pick you up."

I promised to come.

Pulse phoned. He too wanted to see me urgently.

I told him I would be in the hotel at lunch time.

Howard Donovan's car arrived and took me to Encino.

Howard was waiting for me on the steps of the house. His face looked swollen, his eyes were red from lack of sleep, and he mumbled a few words I did not understand. He led me upstairs to Chloe's bedroom, keeping his distance in front of me, as if he were afraid.

He did not enter Chloe's room with me.

The curtains were half-drawn and the sunlight fell at a sharp angle on the red silk cover of a four-poster Spanish bed. Chloe's white face lay on a lacy yellow silk pillow. She looked at me quietly as if her emotion were exhausted.

Her breakfast had been served on a table close to the bed. Silver shone brightly, and the tray was gay with flowers, but the food was untouched.

"Hello," she said. Her voice had a little break in it.

"Feel all right?" I asked, pulling a chair close to the bed.

Chloe looked at me with dark eyes, which made the rest of her face insignificant. Slowly she drew a thin hand from under the covers and with a shy gesture touched mine. Her fingers were cold; her pulse must have been less than sixty. She needed injections of caffeine.

"Who are you?" she asked quietly.

"Dr. Patrick Cory," I said.

She kept on staring at me.

"Last night," she whispered, "you frightened me. You talked like my father. You dragged your left foot. You wrote his name as he did. And you said things only he and I know!"

She smiled, concealing her uneasiness behind the gallantry only breeding produces.

"How did you know about the stamp collection? My father could not have told you that!" she said.

120

"I may have read about it in some magazine," I answered, but she shook her head.

"No."

She fell into deep thought. When she spoke again, it was to herself; she had forgotten my presence.

"I know my father has not died. I knew he would appear again, in his shape or another. I was expecting him!"

She looked at me with a sharp turn of her head, her eyes wide open. "I am sure you told the truth when you said my father had not talked to you. But now he is acting through you!"

She had an explanation of the phenomenon. She took it for granted I too would understand.

"You loved your father?" I asked.

"I hated him," she answered. "And I did think justice had disappeared from the earth because God Himself seemed to be unjust."

She was exalted. Her eyes with their dilated pupils were blank. The world left no image on the retina and she listened to a voice only she could hear.

"You gave Fuller the order to defend Cyril Hinds, but you don't know why!" she said in a quiet triumph.

She suddenly laughed crazily and I expected another fit, but it did not come.

"My father wants to save Cyril Hinds from the hangman's rope, to snatch a life from death in exchange for a life he gave to death! As you might exchange a tin of beef for another, or pay back ten dollars you had borrowed. When I was seven years old, he gave me a lesson in life, his philosophy expressed in a few words: The struggle for money in this world is the struggle for life. The rich man lives a packed life equivalent to many ordinary ones. With hired assistants, slaves, servants, secretaries, sycophants, he accomplishes things in a short time the poor man sometimes takes a year to do. A rich man's life is a hundred times longer than that of a poor man. With money one outlives the others. Money is life itself."

I knew now why she had asked for me so urgently. My strange action of last night convinced her I was sent by fate.

All her life she had suffered her father's domination, waiting for the years of his decline. But he had eluded her by his sudden death. She did not want to believe he was done with living. She wanted him to return! She did not know anything about the brain's artificial life, but she felt it must be!

I moved my right hand, bit my lips, and felt the pain. I was sitting there, not Warren Horace Donovan.

"My father's real name was Dvorak. He came from a small town in Bohemia, in 1895. He changed his name to Donovan, lived in San Juan, and worked in a hardware store. My mother, Katherine, was the owner's daughter, and my father's best and only friend was Roger Hinds, the station master."

Chloe still touched my hand, as if she needed this contact. Suddenly she glanced at me and in a clear voice said: "I've never talked about Roger Hinds to anybody since my mother told me about him. Not even Howard knows. I kept the secret because I loved my mother, nobody else in all my life! Only I, and Roger Hinds, loved her!"

She spoke with undeniable conviction.

I interrupted. I did not want her to lose herself in reminiscence, which had become a dangerous obsession.

"A case of jackknives was unclaimed at the station. Your father bought it, sold the knives to the farmers, and that was the beginning of his mail-order house. I have read about it."

She nodded. "But what the papers did not know was that he began his business with money he borrowed from Roger Hinds, the man my mother loved."

She spoke with a sudden outburst of indignation, as if it had been her own lover and not her mother's.

"Roger admired my father, and my father knew his power over Roger. One day, to ruin him, he asked Roger for a sum of money which he knew Roger did not possess."

"Eighteen hundred and thirty-three dollars and eighteen cents," I said in a flat voice. Chloe nodded impatiently, without wondering at my freakish knowledge.

"It may have been that. Roger took it from the ticket office when my father promised to give it back to him the next day. He trusted Father so implicitly that no feeling of guilt even troubled him. To ruin Roger Hinds, my father purposely held back the money!"

Her voice was as shocked as if this had occurred just yesterday, not forty years ago.

She had derived her strength to live from her resolve to avenge her mother, and since her father died she had nothing to live for. She did not want to believe in his death. She was waiting for some miracle, ready to take refuge in a world remote from our own. Suicide needs purpose and decision; drifting into the unreality of a dream world achieves the same end, easily and more pleasantly.

I had to be careful not to let her excite herself too much with the story she was telling with such conviction.

"Are you sure he did it purposely?" I asked.

"Completely!" Chloe said emphatically. There was no room for doubt in her mind.

"My father wanted to marry and he found his way blocked by Roger. This was a blow to his ego. Whatever, whoever stepped into his path had to be destroyed. He loved Roger as much as he could anyone. He was really very fond of him, but to his dismay Roger was after something he wanted himself! And Donovan felt himself betrayed."

According to Chloe's story, Donovan had deliberately kept the money until an auditor's examination discovered the shortage. Hinds lost his job, and then Donovan returned the sum; he made Roger sign a receipt showing it was he, Donovan, who had saved his friend from going to prison.

When Hinds recovered from the blow, he took a shot at Donovan, whose cheek the scar marked forever. Then, despairing, Hinds hanged himself. He had not told Katherine. He was ashamed of his friend's betrayal.

A few months later Katherine, broken down by Donovan's constant wooing, married him. They left the town at once and settled in Los Angeles.

Some time later she learned the truth. Donovan told her purposely when he found out she still loved Roger.

From this moment he held her by fear. He forced her to bear him children. As one of his possessions, Katherine was not permitted to leave him. He could not stand losing anything which had ever belonged to him.

The woman, her spirit broken, lived a shadowy life. Her

only confidante was her daughter, whose hatred of her own father Katherine nursed.

Several of Katherine's children, conceived in loathing and disgust, had been born dead. Only Howard, the first one, and Chloe, the last, lived. Howard was crushed under his father's fist, never permitted to do anything he had not been ordered to do.

Donovan never gave his son pocket money, and his wife and Chloe never saw cash either. Money is freedom, it makes people independent.

Howard was never given a house key. He had to ring the doorbell like a tradesman, and the servants kept check on his goings and comings. They did not dare cover up for the boy, for they, too, were watched by a set of household spies.

Donovan was omnipresent. He used everybody's eyes and ears for his information. Whoever worked for Donovan gave up his own personality.

When Howard was fifteen he began collecting stamps. To get money to buy them he stole and sold small objects from his father's house—trinkets, silver, spoons, books.

Donovan resented his son's interest in these colored bits of paper, but he tolerated it because the boy convinced him that he was enlarging the collection by clever trading.

When Howard's interest became too absorbing for Donovan's jealousy, he began to compete in his son's field and bought an expensive collection for himself.

Howard possessed a few specimens Donovan did not find in his own album and, without asking permission, he simply took them for his own collection.

At seventeen Howard had the courage to run away. To finance the adventure he stole his father's most valuable stamps. Leaving a letter explaining his reasons, Howard fled to Europe and registered in Paris at the Sorbonne. He studied hard, took his degree in economics, then returned to the States to find a job.

There he lost one position after another. He did not realize that his father was using pressure to force Howard's employers to dismiss him.

Donovan wanted his son back home, and, as always, he got what he wanted.

One day, broke and desperate, Howard returned to his

father's house. Instead of anger, he found Donovan waiting to receive the prodigal with open arms. The embrace was symbolic: he had his son back in his clutches!

From then on, Howard worked for his father without salary or, officially, a position. From time to time Donovan gave him money, like a dole to a poor relative. He never forgave Howard that one independent action. He did not know how to forgive.

But his son had inherited some of Donovan's obstinacy and shrewdness. He intended to beat his father with the only weapon at his command—time! If he waited for his father to grow old, then his time would come. He did wait, silently and patiently. Every day he grew stronger, Donovan older.

When Chloe was fourteen, her mother died. To the girl's surprise, her father took the loss hard. Death had intruded into Donovan's kingdom and taken away one of his possessions without leave. In Donovan's opinon a great injustice had been done him.

For this selfishness Chloe hated him still more. In her eyes he had killed her mother. Chloe wanted revenge for the slow murder and she found a sure way of getting it—by shaming her father's name.

At fourteen she was having affairs with his servants, and cunningly she always saw to it that Donovan found out. Infuriated and hurt, he sent her to girls' schools that were practically prisons, but she always found some way to escape.

When she was sixteen, she married a wrestler, at eighteen a boxer, at nineteen her father's chauffeur.

By then she had conceived the fiendish idea of making herself look more like her mother. She dieted away twenty pounds, had her nose reshaped, and began to be the image of Katherine. She wanted to shock her father with this resemblance. She did not succeed.

Donovan saw through his children's schemes and, once having fathomed their intent, he thought of a counterstroke. The decision was accelerated by the doctor's diagnosis of his incurable illness.

He would disarm his children. He had done only one small thing in his life he regretted, betraying Roger Hinds. If he

125

squared this, what cause could anyone have to hate him? His mind was so primitive that he never was aware of his everyday cruelties.

Donovan considered himself one just man in a treacherous world.

Covering a possible retreat, Donovan had been salting money away for years. He used Hinds's name on this secret account, unconsciously troubled by his feeling of guilt. He liquidated his possessions and gave over his authority to his son. Nobody *took* it away from him!

The next step would have been to make amends to Roger Hinds, who had been buried forty years.

He was searching for Hinds's relatives; he had found only a few. He had it in mind to present them with fortunes, since to him happiness and money were synonymous.

When he found a Hinds in prison, accused of murder, he saw a big chance. Here was a life to be traded back for the one he had snuffed out.

While he was on his way to Geraldine Hinds in Reno, the plane had crashed, and with it he was through playing at fate, for the time being.

While Chloe and I talked, I fitted the pieces of the story together in my mind, made the connections, added missing parts and reasons for the indicated happenings. Obscurities which had baffled me before were cleared. I suddenly knew Horace Donovan better than if I had lived his life, and I was frightened.

He had destroyed everything which opposed his will. Now that death had set up a barrier, his will surmounted it. He was stronger than death!

I saw it all clearly—everything I needed to know for my experiment. The rest asked for only cold analysis, not empiric research.

I must bury this brain ten feet under ground and end its monstrous existence!

"I want Cyril Hinds to die," Choloe blurted out in a hoarse, furious whiser. "He must not go free! Oh no, my father must not have that triumph!"

I smiled at her, put both my hands on hers, and prayed for freedom of thought and will for just this moment.

"Only the things we desire happen to us," I said. "And

as we grow wiser, we can escape some of our instinctive destinies if we will. Don't give that man the homage of your hatred! You have been sensitive to every temper of his. Be sensitive once to your own!"

Chloe turned and looked at me as if she saw me for the first time. Her eyes mirrored a forgotten wish that had been lost in that long struggle. She had found a morbid delight in suffering; her forgotten wish was to find delight in joy.

She stood at the crossroad where the right word would would send her in the right direction and the wrong one into mental chaos.

Bending forward to hold her gaze with all my will-power, I said: "Promise me to get away from here. To Rio, to Buenos Aires. Anywhere where people speak another language and do not talk about your father, only about you, yourself! You are important! Only you! Nobody but you!"

My words seemed to clear away the hate and revenge-fulness. The expression on her pale face, which had been a mask of despair, grew softer. Her lips lost the hard, hurt look.

"Let the pain of life teach you understanding," I said. "And you will not hate life, but, in the joy of understanding, love it."

Chloe smiled, closed her eyes. Her body relaxed.

I held her hand in mine until she fell asleep and her breathing grew easy.

Then I returned to the hotel.

"A gentleman is waiting to see you, sir," the desk clerk said, and he pointed to Yocum, standing in a corner of the lobby.

With a smirk on his thin face, Yocum walked toward me. Flashily dressed in a suit with wide padded shoulders, he wore patent-leather shoes and flourished an expensive gray felt hat with an enormously wide brim.

"Hello, doc," he breezed, and put out his hand in a jovial gesture.

"What do you want?" I asked curtly. The smile on his face spread into a disarming grin.

"Just wanted to show you how I'm getting along!"

His voice had become stronger, for he had been feeding

himself better, but the deep hollows in his cheeks timed the end of his days like an hour-glass. I did not give him more than a few months.

"You ought to be in a sanitarium," I said.

Yocum shrugged his padded shoulders.

"Well—maybe I will! But first I want a little fun. You know, it's like having starved for a long time. I want to eat before I fast again."

He scrutinized me with narrowed eyes, appraising me as if I were a second-hand car.

"You're looking prosperous," he said, satisfied.

The visit had too obvious a purpose.

I took him over to a corner and we sat down. A sudden inspiration flashed through my mind. I might find some use for him!

Yocum crossed his legs carefully, not to crease the pants.

Then he took from his breast pocket a photograph which had been yellowed by smoke. It was the picture of Donovan in the morgue.

"Found it in the ashes of my house," Yocum said casually, showing it and then tucking it away in his coat again.

"What do you want me to do? Buy it?" I asked.

"Don't be unfair, doc," he said arrogantly. "You haven't paid for my house yet!"

I got up without replying, and being a poor crook, he paled.

"Look here, doc," he said threateningly, "I can still sell this picture to Howard Donovan!"

"I wish you would," I replied, and there was so much indifference in my voice Yocum was scared.

"I don't follow," he said, at a loss. "Only a few days ago you were glad to pay for it. . . ."

I sat down again. "I'm tired of you," I said. "You act like an ass that doesn't know when it has gorged itself. Go ahead and tell Donovan! Suppose they do go to Washington Junction and find the brain. What then? You are the one that will go to prison for blackmail!"

"Oh no. Not me!" Yocum said swaggeringly. "You gave me that money willingly."

"Tell it to the judge and see if he believes you. By the way"—I stared at him to frighten him, and succeeded—

"it would be a good idea to have you arrested and get my money back!"

"The money?" he stammered. His face broke into small parts, held together only by the network of deep gray lines. "You can't prove it!"

"I still have your negatives," I said.

"You burned down my house!" He tried to attack me to get me off the offensive.

"Can you prove it? Who will they believe—you or me? You've got a prison record already, haven't you?"

I was hitting in the dark, but I seemed to have struck.

"Photographs!" he murmured. "They won't convict anybody on that evidence."

"You'll have to tell where you got that money for your new suit, and the car you bought. How will you explain? The negatives and the brain in Washington Junction are the only proof!" I said slowly and weightily to make it sink into his consciousness.

He took out the picture again with trembling hands.

"All right, you win," he said tonelessly, and tore it into little pieces. "Forget it, doc."

"Oh no, I won't. You'll hear from me!"

I turned sharply and left him staring helplessly after me. When I turned again, he was gone.

MAY 15

For nearly five months I have discontinued recording these observations. From the moment that Yocum ran out of the Hotel Roosevelt, all my actions have not been my own. My will power was snuffed out like a candle.

A man apparently dead can hear and see, still receive impressions in his mind, but is paralyzed in voice and motion. I was listening and looking on.

To be declared dead while still alive must be the most horrible of all tortures, but there is peace to be found in knowing the worst. I did not know what my body, separated from my mind, was going to do!

I was crying out for help, while my mouth said words I

did not want to say and my hands did things I did not want done. My living brain was trapped.

No message could be sent, no warning given; there was no drug in reach which could bring me respite, no suicide possible, no way of escape.

Donovan's brain dwelt, vampire-like in my body, and no one observed any change in me.

Personality is partly the sum of recollections, and so the brain, remembering only its former existence, went on living its old life. That terse, pithy mind, its actions barbed with the iron of hate and disregard for human life, continued. I, incarcerated, looked on.

I learned to be afraid of the light of day and of the stars of night. I felt I was going insane within the cell of my hermetically sealed existence.

I tried to make a pact with God, if He would let me out of my prison. I had time to pray, and to ponder on my deeds. For even when I seemed asleep, terror kept me awake.

We compute time in minutes and hours, days and years, and measure space in three dimensions, within the physical continuum.

But Donovan's mind existed outside our concrete boundaries. Though inseparable from space, it had a personal concept of time. It seemed to know the future in the same manner as we remember the past. It anticipated coming events, and counteracted them by methods I could not comprehend, for my thinking lacked an understanding of the fourth dimension. I was not aware of impending events.

I am obliged now to identify the brain and my body in Donovan's second existence, as the cerebrum is the seat of the personality and the body only its accidental form.

From that moment on, an impotent spectator, I, Patrick Cory, can only call that freakish, monstrous entity which used my body by its real name: Warren Horace Donovan.

So, a minute after Yocum had run away, Warren Horace Donovan walked out of the hotel, went to Ivar Street and into an office to rent a car. He hired a powerful sedan.

The clerk asked to see his driver's license, and for reasons not known to me until later, Donovan pretended to have left it at home, but he was willing to facilitate the transaction by depositing in cash any sum required.

He signed the papers as Herb Yocum, Kirkwood Drive. If the clerk looked that up in the directory, he must have been satisfied.

Donovan drove the car to a corner behind the hotel, left it there, and took a taxi to Fuller's office. He was limping and a dull pain in his kidneys bothered him.

He looked into the mirror in the taxi. His face was an unhealthy white with a tendency toward yellow. He showed all the indications of a nephritic degeneration of the kidneys. As a man whose leg has been amputated still is nagged by the corn on his missing toe, so Donovan transposed the same sensations he used to feel in his former body into mine.

He went up to the lawyer's office.

After he had waited a few minutes, Fuller came in. His attitude toward Donovan was definitely hostile, but he tried to hide it under a businesslike manner.

Donovan followed him to the library, where they sat down.

Fuller opened the conversation grimly. "I wish you would explain your strange behavior last night in Howard's house. I don't understand that kind of humor."

"I'm not asking for your opinion of any of my actions, Fuller," Donovan replied acidly. "You're paid to get Hinds out of prison, not to criticize my conduct!"

Fuller's face flushed, but he spoke in his pleasant conference voice: "Well, I'm not so sure if I want to take over this case at all. It's hopeless. The man is a cold-blooded murderer. You'd better give it to somebody else."

Donovan grunted, got up, opened the small cupboard near the door. In it, connected to an electric circuit, was a switch. Donovan snapped it off and limped back to the table.

Fuller watched, his features distorted. He sensed a more than natural intelligence behind Donovan's strange behavior, but he could not define it.

"Always careful, aren't you?" Donovan said, and his voice was threatening. Fuller looked at him with veiled fear.

"How did you know?" he began.

"Never mind," Donovan cut him short. "I don't want my conversations recorded. You won't walk out on me, either! Just remember the Ralston and Trueman case. We

131

don't need to fence with each other." He used Fuller's expression of the night before.

Fuller paled as if he were going to faint. A hideous fear seemed to possess him.

Donovan went on with sardonic determination: "Pulse tried to blackmail me. You'd better see that he comes down in his price. Tell him I want to talk to him. At once!"

Fuller looked dazed. He did not dare fight back, picked up the telephone, and told the switchboard girl. He took his time talking. When he hung up he seemed to have himself in control again.

"The district attorney is keeping back a surprise witness," he said, and gave Donovan a quick glance of inquiry. "If he calls that one we're in bad shape."

"Then don't let him call that witness," Donovan said in quiet anger.

Fuller bent forward over the glass table, beads of sweat standing out over his forehead.

"You can't pervert justice," he said in a low, desperate voice. "There are things you can't do. You just can't!"

"But *you* can!" Donovan said cruelly. "I want Hinds freed."

He was a maniac with a fixed idea. No one in the world could have deviated Donovan from his course, but Fuller was not aware of that. He went on fighting.

"What interest have you in that man? You're not related to him. You never saw him before!"

"It's no business of yours," Donovan said aloofly. "Just get him free!"

"But this witness can't be bought," Fuller said in despair.

"I'll pay as much as he wants," Donovan answered.

"It's a girl, only thirteen years old. I can't approach her to take money for telling a lie! She would not understand."

The misery in Fuller's voice was heart-rending.

They sat quiet until Fuller continued, exasperated:

"She is a little girl from San Francisco, who ran away from home to break into the movies. Hitch-hiked here and had no place to sleep. She was hiding in the entrance of a building when Hinds ran over the old woman. She saw him do it. She saw him stop and drive back in reverse. The old woman recognized him and cried out his name. 'Cyril!' she cried, and begged him to call a doctor. But Hinds backed up farther and ran over her face."

Fuller spoke as if that were evidence directed against Donovan.

"And she did not go to the police?" Donovan said.

"She was afraid of being sent home," Fuller answered, the lawyer again, his voice soft and pleading. "She lives at the Loma Street Y.W.C.A."

"Then get her parents out here. You can talk to them, can't you?"

"They are here," Fuller said.

"All right! Pay them whatever you want to take the girl across the state border. She must not be found for the next year. Then the district attorney will have no witness, and we are in the clear," Donovan said. "A young girl who runs away from home is not a trustworthy witness anyway. She is hysterical and likely to imagine things."

"But she heard the old woman call him Cyril!" Fuller was still persistent.

Donovan got up, impatient.

"She read that in the papers! Must I tell you how to get elements of doubt into this? Am I the lawyer in the case? I see I am obliged to take things into my own hands."

He limped to the door. Fuller followed him.

"See that the girl is taken back to her parents. You're an idiot, Fuller. You're slipping!"

Donovan walked out.

Fuller did not dare reply.

I, mute witness of the scene, wanted to cry out. Fuller might hear me. . . . But I had no mouth to make myself heard. I was nothing but a brain in a vessel.

Pulse, who was just entering the waiting-room, strode over to Donovan and whispered with ponderous alertness: "Hello, Dr. Cory. I was coming to see you at the hotel when Fuller phoned me."

Looking quickly at the lawyer from under his heavy eyelids, Pulse continued in his low voice: "I just saw the girl's family. . . ."

"All right, let's get going," Donovan interrupted gruffly, and limped out of the room. "Come with me, Pulse."

The big man turned quickly, shocked by Donovan's

abruptness. He always expected to be treated with the same politeness he used to lubricate his affairs, but he ran after Donovan and caught up with him in the elevator.

"Got a car with you?" Donovan asked.

Pulse nodded, cowed into a submission which he could not explain.

"Drive me to where that girl's father is staying," Donovan ordered when they had reached the car.

Pulse squeezed his gross body behind the steering wheel. "The situation is very delicate," he said warningly. "The man is a minister."

"I've heard of the church taking money," Donovan said. "They even sold Christ for a price!"

Pulse was shocked beyond words, his large, fluid eyes fixed on Donovan. "I wish you would not bring religion into this business." His voice was suddenly full and resonant. "We should grope after goodness as we grope after wisdom."

"Listen to him. He's just been talking to a minister!" Donovan jeered. "Just take me to him and I'll show you whether he'll take money! He'd be the first one who didn't. The price tag on religious people is just a little higher, that's all. You're religious, aren't you, Pulse?"

Pulse did not reply. His glasses slid down his nose, and he pushed them back with an angry gesture.

"Things you wouldn't do for a cigar!" Donovan finished contemptuously.

That must have reminded Pulse of the money he expected to be paid, because he said quietly and docilely: "We have five 'pills' in our box already, Dr. Cory. Five jurors on our side! We're pretty much on the safe side now."

"Not so long as that girl is around," Donovan muttered. "We must get her out of the way."

He stared in front of him blankly, wrapped in thoughts which seemed far in the future.

"Go on. Quick!" Donovan suddenly shouted. "Fast, man!"

Pulse, shocked into activity, pressed down the accelerator, and the car shot forward along the broad Beverly Boulevard.

"The girl's father lives at the Weatherby Apartments on

134

Van Ness," Pulse said. Donovan did not seem to be listening. He kept on staring, sitting there motionless.

In my mental prison, I felt a nameless fear, which increased the nearer we got to Van Ness. I knew I was going insane; the clearness of my thinking began to dim.

The hope that the spell would be broken and I would again be in command of my own body suddenly dissolved into a screaming despair.

If only Schratt would kill that brain! Overturn the vessel in which it swam! Or cut off the electric current which kept it alive!

Schratt must be aware what I was going through. The encephalograph must have shown strange new signs, which he, the scientist, should have been able to interpret.

But he, too, might be out of action, ruled by the brain as I was!

"Here," Pulse said, pointing at a big white building.

"Stop the car," Donovan ordered, "and get out from behind that wheel!"

Pulse looked up, surprised, but then he consented, and while Donovan slid into the driver's seat, Pulse walked around the car and got in beside him.

"What are we waiting for, Dr. Cory?" Pulse asked, suddenly apprehensive.

He could not understand Donovan's strange behavior, first rushing him, now waiting. Donovan did not reply; he kept staring ahead of him. His features must have had a frightening expression, which was mirrored in those of Pulse.

"Why don't we go inside and see the girl's father? I can introduce you and maybe he'll listen to you."

No reply. Pulse moved uneasily in his seat.

The street was deserted.

A couple of people came out of the apartment house, one an elderly woman dressed in black, the other a pale, pretty girl of about thirteen.

Suddenly Donovan stirred, stepped on the gas, and the car jerked under the clutch. Its front wheels jumped the sidewalk. It shot straight toward the two women.

For a second Pulse was petrified; then he gave a hoarse cry of despair. His fat hand grabbed the steering wheel and he swung the car off the sidewalk. The coupé nearly turned over. Pirouetting on squeaking tires, it swerved, turned itself around, and then shot toward Melrose Avenue.

"Stop this car!" Pulse moaned. He looked bleary and there were heavy rings under his eyes.

Donovan cut off the engine.

"You nearly killed them," Pulse said. His shock suddenly turned into a crying rage. "You tried to murder them! You wanted to kill that girl!" He ran out of breath.

Donovan stepped out of the car.

"We must get rid of her," he said slowly, like a man in a trance, and walked away.

"Not with my car!" Pulse shouted after him hysterically. "Not with my car!"

He stared at Donovan with tears streaming down his face.

Donovan walked on, limping. He hailed a taxi and said: "The Roosevelt Hotel."

He sank onto the seat, breathing heavily, staring in front of him, holding his sides above the kidneys with both hands.

Suddenly he knocked at the glass partition.

The driver stopped.

Donovan went into a liquor store and bought a quart of gin, which he hid in his pocket.

Then he had himself driven back to the hotel.

I saw Janice the moment Donovan entered the lobby. He saw her too, but he passed her without any sign of recognition.

Janice had turned sharply. She took two quick steps in his direction, then hesitated, stopped by an intangible doubt. She watched him as he limped to the elevator, presumably puzzled that he moved so differently from me, with the step of an old, sick man.

Donovan went upstairs to the room, sat on the bed motionless, and waited.

He knew she would come.

I was praying for her to come in.

I could heardly bear the tension any longer. I wanted to cry, to shout, to sob. Then, in a last effort at sanity, I collected my strength to be able to concentrate on her, to make myself understand.

Janice knocked.

"Come in," Donovan shouted.

Janice stood in the doorway as in a picture frame. She stared at Donovan with wide blue eyes, and when he did not ask her to come in, she closed the door behind her.

She has that indefinable intuition which can understand happenings outside everyday reality. Surely she would realize that it was not I, Patrick Cory, sitting on this bed, but Warren Horace Donovan.

"Patrick," she said softly, and her voice was strained with uncertainty. Her eyes grew so dark the pupils were imperceivable.

She stood motionless. Her subconscious fear, which she controlled with singular bravery, gave her an untouchable, aloof air. She was not capable of fright. The more horrible the truth, the braver she would be. She stood taller than the mounting danger.

She wore her bravery like an armor, and an air of virginity made her still less conquerable.

She gazed at Donovan with singular fixity.

"What do you want?" Donovan asked gruffly, and for the first time I knew the brain was afraid. It trembled, threatened by something intangibly stronger than itself. It was evil opposed.

She could only divine the strange change which had taken place in my body, but she knew the influence the brain had on me. Nobody who had not experienced it could imagine the brain's power, but Janice did not need to be told. Clairvoyance is commonplace to those who have it and she knew.

I tried to call her. I tried to tell her that there in the writing-desk lay the case history of Donovan. Being a doctor's wife she would think of that, and find it. She had to find it, to read it, to be able to understand that the monster I had created must be destroyed.

I shouted within my prison and, as if she had heard me, a shiver of fear shook her. But only for a second, and I could not be sure that she had understood.

"What do you want?" Donovan asked again.

She smiled disarmingly. "To stay with you. I thought you might need me."

"Don't run after me," Donovan answered. "I don't want

to see you around here any more. Go home to your mother. Go wherever you like. But leave me alone."

His voice was without inflection, as people speak who are suffering physically. She recognized that and stepped closer.

"You are in pain," she said.

Donovan jumped up and walked toward her. "Get out of here," he shouted. "*Out!* Can't you understand?"

He stepped in front of her and she looked into his eyes, searchingly, as if she would read the truth in them.

He met her gaze for a few seconds, then turned away.

"Go on, get out!" he said hoarsely.

The door closed behind her.

My mind became suddenly quiet.

Now that I was sure she knew, I trusted her implicitly. All these years while she had lived close to me, she knew me so well, reading my thoughts before I was conscious of them myself, being there when I wanted her, and away when I wished to be alone. She was my thinking shadow.

All these years had been only a preparation for the great task, which, she knew, would ask one day for all her strength. Here it was. How could she fail me?

A bond exists between certain people which may bring death when it breaks. Two persons connected by those immaterial links might not be in love with each other, might hate each other even, but still a strange identification which cannot be put down in formulas binds them together. An abstract identification lying outside space and time.

Often these persons are not aware of the bond until a great disaster or a threat of extreme danger breaks down the barriers of their ignorance. In these moments we step over the threshold of the unknown world and use weapons we were not aware of before.

Donovan sat down on the bed again. With a sigh he opened the bottle of gin he had hidden under the pillow. He swallowed the liquid in great gulps. He wanted to get drunk, to drown his imaginary pains.

Taking heavy pulls from the bottle on his way, he got up again and locked the door.

If he got drunk enough, I would be free! Then I could call Janice. I could call anyone in the world for help!

But suddenly I realized it was I who was drunk, not Donovan! He lived in my body, but the nerves of my stomach influenced my brain, not his! The drink had affected me, not him!

I felt dizzy and the room began to swim.

Donovan went on emptying the bottle.

I seldom touch alcohol, for I hate that fogginess of mind, that loss of the control over my body. Now I felt how I was losing consciousness, my mind being blotted out, but in my drunkenness the fear came back and the doubts that Janice might not have understood.

Donovan emptied the bottle hastily, eagerly, waiting for the alcohol to take effect. I was vaguely conscious of his surprise when he found himself still sober.

Then, like a man falling into a stagnant pool, I lost consciousness.

I do not know for how long I slept, but a sudden terrifying premonition of approaching death tore me out of my drunken sleep.

I sat up in bed in full command of my body!

For the first time in days I could move my limbs at my own will. Like a man in the death house who unexpectedly finds the door open and the guards away, I was free. Donovan had left me.

I swung my feet out of bed, but I was too drunk to stand up.

I tried to crawl to the door. Prompted by that terrifying premonition of danger, I had to call Janice while Donovan was away.

But I was paralyzed. The alcohol in my blood halted the movements of my muscles. When I tried to pick myself up, my arms gave way and I fell flat on my face, hitting the rug, which was soft and smelled of disinfectant.

As I lay prostrate, I only remembered that I must move. I had forgotten why. The sense of mortal danger remained, but my body stayed fixed to the rug.

I was caught again. Donovan's brain returned.

When the telephone rang, much later, I was in bed, and it was still dark night.

Donovan switched on the small lamp and picked up the receiver.

It was Schratt.

"Patrick?" he asked in a terrified voice.

Donovan did not answer and Schratt repeated his question.

"Yes," Donovan finally said, as if he knew what Schratt wanted to tell him.

"A man broke into the laboratory," Schratt cried. "He tried to attack the brain. I heard him shouting for help while I was in bed!"

Schratt stopped, overcome by excitement.

"Yes," Donovan repeated. It was an affirmation, not a question.

"He is dead," Schratt reported hoarsely. "Collapsed when he touched the vessel. When I came in, he was already dead."

"Yes," Donovan said again, without emotion.

Schratt shouted: "The brain murdered him. The heart stopped, as if he had died of coronary thrombosis. He had the pallor that follows cyanosis and apprehensive anguish of death. But how can that be? Did he die under hypnotic command? It can't be possible! The brain can kill! It is too horrible to imagine!"

His voice faltered and I in my mental cell became petrified. If the brain could kill from a distance, nobody had a chance to stop it from living!

Donovan was holding the telephone without uttering a word.

"Are you listening?" Schratt's desperate voice came through again.

"Yes," Donovan said quietly.

"Who was that man? How did it happen he knew about the brain? Why did he break into the house? I found his name. He had a driver's license on him. . . . Do you know him? His name is . . ."

"Yocum!" Donovan finished Schratt's sentence impatiently. "Just forget about him. Only a cheap little chiseler. He should have stayed in his own back yard. I'm glad he's dead!"

"What did you say?" Schratt shouted, not believing his ears.

"Send him to the morgue. He was due there anyhow."

When Donovan put down the receiver, I could hear Schratt still shouting into the phone.

Donovan switched out the lamp and lay still.

The first streak of pale morning streaked through the blinds.

Now I understand why the brain had left me for a few minutes. To murder Yocum. It had had to defend itself and needed all its will-power to kill.

After it had murdered, it projected itself back into me. Yocum wanted to destroy the evidence of his blackmail, the brain. This was what I had wanted him to do when I threatened him with arrest.

I did not know the brain could kill without using anyone's hands. I had not meant for Yocum to die!

Again the telephone shrilled. It was Schratt.

"What's the matter now?" Donovan asked, annoyed.

Schratt must have lost all his control.

"The encephalograph shows strange reactions," he said. "I just wanted you to know. It jumps in dots. The electric energy shows up in explosions on the strip."

"I am tired, I want to sleep." Donovan cut him short, ending the conversation.

I became so frightened, my mind blacked out for several minutes.

The potentialities of the brain had no limits!

"Brain-power is unpredictable," Schratt had warned me once. Where would it end?

Janice might try something foolish. As Yocum had. Schratt would warn her. I was sure he kept in contact with her.

But if he did not—that would be her death! The brain would get rid of her as it had destroyed everything which stood in its way.

Janice had to be warned. How could I do it?

Maybe the brain could read my thoughts—thoughts created in the same cerebrum that served its consciousness. It might already be spying on me, amused at my impotence.

It might find a fiendish pleasure in teasing me with its cruelty.

I suddenly had the terrible thought that it might make love to Janice. Janice was pretty. And Donovan was Patrick in her eyes!

If that happened, I would be the onlooker! Betrayed with my own body!

Was I insane?

I had to be quiet, thinking clearly, thinking clearly, thinking clearly! Thinking of Janice. She would not lose her head, she never did. She believed in me and I could not disappoint her. I, Patrick Cory, could not become mentally deranged, crazed by fear. She would never forgive me, she would despise me.

I had only to have patience. My moment would come. I had only to wait and to remember Janice, who did not want me to lose my mind.

In the morning Donovan surprised me by quoting the mysterious line: "Amidst the mists . . ." as if, in his sleep, those words had tortured him too.

Donovan had changed in appearance since Yocum's death. His face had hardened, his mouth had become thinner, the eyes were glaring and inhuman. Ontogeny, his personal experience, was reshaping my features.

I watched him with my innate curiosity, in a sudden reaction of fearless interest, as if I were able still to record on paper the concrete facts of my scientific observation.

The dreadful moments of terror and desperation had grown fewer. I was drifting through the center of the mental typhoon, but the big storm was to come.

As a man in the hour preceding his death has no apprehension of his impending end, but, on the contrary, is filled with new hope for a future life, so I watched that reflection of mine, which looked at itself in the mirror, the face immobile, pale, the hair graying, lines deep-bitten around its nostrils.

It was I, but at the same time not I at all! That face in there had aged during the last days. It was not the face of a man of thirty-eight any more, but of a man haunted by weary age and impending death.

Donovan talked to himself in a Slavic language, which I

could not understand. He finished dressing, went out, stepped into his rented car, which still stood at the corner behind the hotel where he had left it days ago.

He drove toward Beverly Boulevard and then to Van Ness. A few hundred feet from the Weatherby Apartments he stopped the car, folded his arms, and sat staring motionlessly ahead.

He was waiting for the girl to appear. Again he intended to kill her.

Donovan would never have acted in this manner when he was alive in his own body. But what chance did the brain take? If it murdered, it was I who would go to the electric chair! It was I who would have to die, not this brain.

It could continue its parasitic life in any other body, perhaps Schratt's or Sternli's. Or a woman's, or a child's. Or, if it chose, a dog's! There was no limit to its polymorphism.

I did not know if the brain had ever entertained these considerations in its diseased imagination. It behaved as if only its thalamus was working, without the restraining influence of the cortex.

People whose thalamus has been separated from the rest of the brain by surgical operation have no control. They become unpredictable, dangerous. Donovan's brain acted precisely this way.

Donovan himself had never had a pronounced sense of ethics, but still he was forced to submit to the laws of society. The brain had lost all ability to distinguish right from wrong now.

It had only the one idea, the one Donovan had died with: to make good for Roger Hinds's death. It pursued that objective without restraint. Murder was only a means to achieve its objective. The brain was running amok!

A police car drove up the street followed by a black limousine. Both cars stopped in front of the apartment house and two men went in, to return after a few minutes with the girl and her mother. Frightened by the strange abortive attempt on her life, the parents had asked for police protection.

Traveling slowly down the street, the police car had spotted Donovan. It stopped alongside.

Elaborately Donovan took an Upman from his pocket and lighted it.

"Do you live here?" the police officer called suspiciously through the window.

"No." Donovan shook his head.

"What are you doing?" the policeman asked.

"Lighting a cigar!" Donovan answered, friendly.

One policeman stepped from the car, while the driver stayed ready to back him up in an emergency.

"Didn't I see you around here yesterday?" The officer was looking the car over.

"No." Donovan smiled.

"It was a coupé," the driver called.

"Your license!" The officer stamped his heavy boot on the running board. Donovan took the wallet out of his pocket and opened it.

"Dr. Patrick Cory, Washington Junction, Arizona," the officer read. He relaxed his suspicion. "What are you doing here, doc?"

"Going downtown to see my lawyer. But it's early, so I stopped to smoke a cigar. Anything wrong with that?" Donovan answered dryly.

"No, nothing. But you'd better drive along," the officer ordered cryptically.

Donovan pressed the accelerator slowly, cursing under his breath in the language I did not understand. In the back mirror he saw the officer was taking the license number.

His plan had failed.

On Sunset Boulevard Donovan stopped at a hardware store to buy a strong thin rope, a long heavy kitchen knife, and a trunk, which he had put in his car.

Fear gripped me again. What did he want with a knife and a rope? Whom did he intend to hide in that trunk?

He parked the car in front of the hotel.

Sitting in a chair in the lobby, Sternli waited. His kind old face beamed when he saw Donovan enter, and he hurried over with a happy smile.

"Dr. Cory!" Then he became aware of the change which had occurred in that face. "Are you ill?" He was deeply concerned.

144

Donovan looked at him with faint indignation. "Certainly not. No! What makes you think so? But you look rather dilapidated."

Sternli looked at him stupidly. He was so confused that he brought his thick glasses closer to Donovan's face to make sure he was talking to the right man.

Donovan spoke impatiently. "Did you see Geraldine Hinds? And that plumber in Seattle?"

Sternli answered slowly with a presentiment of evil. He apprehended that strange similarity to his former master, which was not found in a likeness of features, but in similarity of behavior. By the evidence of his eyes it was Dr. Patrick Cory to whom he spoke.

"I wrote a report. The cases are quite uncomplicated."

"Give it to me." Donovan held out his hand.

Sternli seemed surprised at Donovan's urgency. He opened the brief-case and took out a few typewritten pages.

"Geraldine Hinds runs a boarding house in Reno. She is comparatively well off. But the plumber in Seattle is very poor. Well, with a little money they could both be made very happy."

"Just give me the facts," Donovan said gruffly.

He grabbed the papers and left the old man standing there alone.

"Send up your expense sheet. I'd like to know how much you spent on the trip," he called back over his shoulder, limping away.

Sternli stared after him. His face looked haunted. He looked after Donovan, recognizing him for a ghost!

Donovan went quickly to his room, with the papers in his hand. He opened the door, limped over to the writing-desk, and pulled out the middle drawer.

He froze in his motion. My diary was not there!

He sat down for a while, his head bowed, listening to a message only he could hear.

No doubt Janice had taken the diary as I wanted her to do.

Having learned by now the circumstances and the dangers, she would be careful not to expose herself. I was praying that she had gone beyond Donovan's reach.

Suddenly Donovan gave a long gasp as if some terrifying

message had reached him. Like a blind man he groped his way to the telephone. He sat on his bed, his hands on his lap, and talked to himself in his strange language.

The telephone rang. It was Fuller. "No. She hasn't been here, Dr. Cory!"

"All right," Donovan answered, impersonally.

"Everything is going fine," Fuller added hastily, to cover his lie. "I've laid out a strong defense for Cyril Hinds. Saw him today. Tomorrow I'll give him the answers to rehearse."

"All right," Donovan said, without expression.

"About that girl," Fuller continued with forced optimism. "Well, I've decided she isn't dangerous at all. She's so scared already, the jury won't take her seriously. She isn't even sure she heard or saw now."

"All right," Donovan replied. I was aware he was not listening at all.

"Why don't you come over and have lunch with me? We can discuss a few points I don't want to mention on the phone. Pulse will be here . . ." Fuller hesitated. Pulse certainly had informed him of the attempted murder. Not mentioning it at all, Fuller must have some trick up his sleeve.

"All right," Donovan said.

"And please bring Mrs. Cory with you. I would like to meet her."

"All right." Donovan put back the receiver.

He stood like a statue. Suddenly he began to tremble, swaying to and fro without changing his position. Only his hands opened and closed, burying the fingernails deep in the palms.

Staggering, he walked out of his room, limped down the corridor, and knocked at Janice's door.

"Who is it?" she asked in a high, childish voice. She had not run to safety!

"Open up," Donovan ordered.

"The door is unlocked," she replied.

Janice sat on the bed, her feet tucked under her and my journal in her lap. With strangely quiet eyes she looked at Donovan as if she were trying to see right into his brain, but she made no attempt to hide the book she was holding.

"Hello." She spoke in a light voice without changing her position. She seemed anxious to have him see the journal, which she had taken without his permission.

She hoped he would talk about it, but he only said: "I want you to come with me."

She nodded, never taking her eyes off his face. A small frozen smile around her lips betrayed that she was not as much at ease as she wished to appear.

Ostentatiously she closed the diary, then crossed to put it in the desk, which she locked carefully. She picked up her handbag and hid the key in it.

Again she waited, hoping Donovan would talk to her.

I could not guess what Janice was thinking. She must have known that it was fatal to follow Donovan. She must also, having read my report, have known it was the brain, not I, that directed my body. But for some reason I could not divine, she ran headlong into danger.

"Let's go." She took her hat and coat and walked out into the corridor in front of Donovan.

If only I could have held her back! She was going to her death! Janice trusted her own strength foolishly. There was not strength enough in anyone to resist Donovan.

As she passed the desk, she dropped her key and told the clerk she would be back soon.

Donovan walked to the car and she followed him to the door.

"Where did you get the Buick?" she asked, hesitating a moment as if to gain a small respite.

"Rented," Donovan murmured.

She stepped inside. Donovan drove off.

On Highland Avenue he turned north.

"Where are we going?" Janice asked. Her voice was calm.

"I have to talk to you," he said, as if that were sufficient answer to her question.

On Woodrow Wilson Drive he turned into the hills, and up an unpaved road, then stopped the car on a wide deserted plateau where years ago a real-estate agent had planned to build a big hotel.

Like a huge spider's web the town sprawled in all directions. The wind carried up the subdued hum of the busy city. Cars hooted, the street cars thundered, all far away and mixed with a deep murmur as of thousands of voices.

The horizon was pale blue where the land met the ocean, and dark oil derricks stood on their thin legs against the sky.

Donovan cut off the engine, slowly turned his head, and looked at the trunk in the rear seat, then turned back like an automaton.

Janice followed his movement, and I was aware that all the time she had realized her danger. But she had never run away from anything, and she did not run away from this moment either.

"Why do you want to kill me?" she asked quietly, almost curiously.

"I can't let anybody stand in my way," Donovan murmured, but turned his face aside, not to meet her eyes. "The world is against me. Everybody is against me." There was no bitterness in his voice, and he spoke without emotion, as if he related plain facts.

"Nobody is against you," Janice said. She put her hand on his shoulder firmly, to make him look at her. "You always saw the world in the wrong focus. All your life you believed people were against you, and it was not true. Believe me! It was just an obsession. You confused cause and effect."

Donovan listened. For the first time someone talked to him so straightforwardly. He seemed astonished and interested. This was what Janice wanted to try, attacking Donovan with the truth. She went on talking to that monster believing she could approach him with logic.

I saw her danger, and her gallant useless sacrifices.

"All your life it was you who attacked people first," Janice continued. "And when they fought back—sometimes for their lives—you were amazed. You considered yourself attacked without reason. Whoever opposed you wronged you. You never understood that one's desires must be controlled. Life is a mutual compromise. If you would only understand that simple law, which makes it possible for society to exist, you would not have been so unhappy. Nobody ever wanted to harm you."

He listened to her plea, but he did not understand. He was emotionless, like a road machine which pushes boulders out of its way.

148

Janice swayed a little and her eyes became vacant. With all her will-power and love she was trying to tip the scale of this insane mind.

"If you would only love, the love would come back to you," Janice said.

She saw me, Patrick, sitting beside her. She only believed that Donovan's and my personalities had become confused. Now she wanted Donovan to disappear and Patrick to answer. She believed her will and mine, united, were strong enough to break that freakish telepathic paralysis which robbed me of the use of my own sensory system.

She knew I was listening and suddenly, feeling that she fought a losing battle, she appealed to me directly: "Patrick! You can be free if you have faith. Help me!"

"I am not Patrick," Donovan said.

In his eyes she must have read her doom. Donovan muttered again, swallowing half of his words. There was desperation in his expression, and rage against Janice.

"Why do you interfere with me? You want to make me unhappy, as all of them made me unhappy. Everybody is against me. But you won't stop me!"

He raised his hands and for a moment Janice trembled in a vague, horrible fear.

"No," she said.

She seemed to diminish in stature, but still she did not move.

Donovan's hands shot out, but only got hold of her coat. She had pushed the door open and jumped out of the car. She ran.

She did not shout for help.

Then she stopped and waited.

Donovan followed her slowly.

She looked like a child, her brown hair swept by the strong loud wind that blew gray dust over the flat hilltop.

He must have looked like a lunatic as he closed in on her. His right hand held the knife. The other swung the rope.

Janice did not retreat. She held him with her steady blue eyes as if she could will him to keep his distance.

When he lifted the knife, she hit his wrist with the flat of her hand. As a nurse she had been trained to defend herself against the insane.

I cried out her name, but I could not make her hear. I, who wanted to stop that beast, would have to look on at the murder!

She made him drop the knife, but he lashed her across the face with the rope, and as she staggered, he caught her and grabbed her throat with his right hand. She was no match for him.

I stammered a prayer. "Faith!" Janice had said.

I could not think clearly any more. I was in a burning hell, staring into her thin helpless face, as my hand bent her head back to the ground.

Suddenly I was conscious of the muscles of my shoulders and the pain in my wrist where Janice had hit. I was breathing, moving. Like the tide running off from a steep beach, Donovan's personality flowed away, and I, Patrick Cory, returned into my own body!

I released her throat. When the grip relaxed, she did not faint. I held her in my arms, looking into her poor, pale face. Her eyes, still steady and defiant, met mine, and in their depths I saw a fear that vanished.

She must have recognized me instantly, for she gasped my name and closed her arms around me.

I lifted her up and kissed her. I stammered, not knowing what I said. I only knew I was free.

We sank down on the dusty ground together, both exhausted. She held me tight, her head close to my chest as if she were listening to my heart beat.

We could not talk.

Slowly my senses returned, and I lifted her to her feet. "Quick!" I said in terror. "Take the car and drive away. Before he returns!"

She looked into my eyes and, prompted by her clairvoyance, she said with a smile: "He will never come back."

I drove to the highway.

While dozens of cars passed us, we stopped, too exhausted to move, waiting for our strength to return.

At the next service station I put through a long-distance call to Washington Junction.

I heard the telephone ring for a long time, but Schratt did not answer.

IN front of me lie a few handwritten pages, a report by Schratt. Janice brought it in today. She did not want to give it to me before, but she thinks I should read it now.

When I look out of my room—Janice has pushed the bed to the window—I can see the garden of the Phoenix hospital with its palm trees. Convalescents wander along the narrow garden paths. Some just sit in the sun, some are still in wheel chairs.

In a few days I will be down there too.

I shall have some difficulty reading Schratt's report. His writing is hieroglyphic, jotted down in terrific haste. Sometimes he forgot to date the entry.

Janice offered to transcribe it, but I wanted to read it from Schratt's own hand.

Schratt wrote:

THE futility of psychology to account for mental reactions is due to an attempt to explain everything in terms of consciousness. Donovan's actions cannot be judged that way. His sphere of mind is not coextensive with the sphere of his consciousness. His thought process is an imperfect, disjointed series of feelings, all pointing to an abstract goal.

He is insane, measured by the common conception, and he must be treated as an incurable lunatic. Patrick's method of trying to explore this mind, which is not rational, can end only in disaster.

The borderline between lunacy and genius is not to be precisely defined, but it is my contention that exactly at the moment Donovan's brain began to influence Patrick's Patrick too crossed that borderline. He cannot be considered a normal person. A good scientist should have been aware of his own limitations, and not have transgressed into the unexplorable. Deluded by his own seeming ingeniousness, Patrick cannot see facts clearly any longer.

Granting that ideas are the sole reality in experimentation, their practical use has to be restrained.

Watching and weighing this dangerous experiment, I see clearly now that nothing valuable has been added to Donovan's brain. Only its bad concepts, its criminal instincts, its undesirable reflexes have been strengthened, until they have reached monstrous proportions.

For years I have known the dangers latent in Patrick's impetuous desire for dangerous experiments. Having warned him frequently, I have only one course left; I must interfere with the progress of this experiment before it is too late.

Patrick's intelligence is superior to mine. I cannot fight him with arguments or reasons. To stop him, I shall have to deceive him.

The moment of my decision came when Patrick tried to kill me, following a telepathic order of this insane piece of flesh which he keeps preserved in the vessel.

Afterward it was not difficult to convince him I honestly wanted to assist him. The brain itself helped to persuade him to go.

Patrick left Washington Junction on the 21st of November.

I am in charge of the brain. Truly an irony. It appointed its own killer! But at that time the brain could not read my thoughts. Since then it has gained so much power I would not dare suggest my help at this point.

To protect myself from giving away my intention to the brain, I use a very simple trick. I remember a silly tongue-twister I learned as a child. My mother practiced it with me to cure me of a lisp. Now I repeat the lines incessantly whenever the lamp is burning and the brain awake. "Amidst the mists and coldest frosts he thrusts his fists against the posts and still insists he sees the ghosts!"

While I say this sentence continuously, no thought can possibly enter my brain.

I have connected a buzzer with the lamp to warn me if I should ever overlook the light and go on writing when the brain is awake.

It is disturbed by this stereotypic repetition. The encephalograph clearly shows delta curves. This proves that the brain can read my thoughts. My precaution was taken none too soon.

Janice phoned me from Los Angeles. Patrick had talked to her. She told me about their conversation and asked my advice. I cannot give her instructions. I cannot take the risk of any other mind's knowing what I intend to do. Janice never was Patrick's confidante, and now she must think she has lost me too. That makes me sad.

Tonight Patrick phoned. He wants to return home. I persuaded him to stay where he is. My mission has failed if he comes back.

To destroy the brain I must proceed carefully, with the precision a difficult test requires, for I am ignorant of the brain's potential powers.

Theoretically it is easy to destroy the brain. I should have only to stop feeding it, to cut off the electricity, to upset the vessel. I could poison the brain; a grain of potassium cyanide in the blood serum would kill it. Except that it might sense my purpose in advance and strike first. How, I do not know, but if it has that power, my plan would fail.

I cannot take a risk. I must wait, employ the safest method. In the meantime I must go on as the brain's faithful servant. Must nurse it, take its temperature, read the encephalograph.

It looks horrible. A whitish-gray, formless mass, which grows to the edge of its container. I would not be surprised if it suddenly developed eyes and ears and a mouth! It is monstrous!

DECEMBER 5

Janice arrived today without having announced her coming.

She acted very nervous. I sat opposite her in her bedroom listening to what she had to say about Patrick's strange behavior and knew all the answers without being able to tell her anything. I was fearful the brain might read my thoughts, so I talked lightly to her, and advised her to forget about Patrick for a while. Why not go back to her mother?

But she was returning to Los Angeles; she knew Patrick would need her soon. For a moment she even convinced me that this was the right thing for her to do, but I would not tell her so.

She was upset, thinking I took Patrick's side against her! She believed I had deserted her!

Desert Janice? She was blind, or she would have known the unkindness of her words.

She asked me many questions and I had to lie, without even daring to let her guess the truth. She left me soon.

It was a sad day for me, but I was consoled to think she would understand later.

DECEMBER 13

THE situation has become reversed. Patrick phoned to order me to stop feeding the brain. He is frightened! He wants it to die, but too late. I had to refuse.

How could I agree when it might have meant my own life, might have been beyond my power to do what he wanted? If the brain should switch its telepathic force to me instead of Patrick, I shall have to carry out its orders.

I have always groped for life's hidden meaning, and I know now! Life trained me for this task. I am thinking clearly, as I never did before. My years have not been wasted. I believe in no one religion, I believe in them all, for the search for God is a personal undertaking.

One day Patrick will know and understand, for knowledge comes from within.

I know, I understand!

MISSED my chance to kill it!

A man broke into the laboratory today and attacked the brain with a wrench. The sudden attack distracted its attention. That was the time for me to kill! Something violent must happen; then it can be destroyed.

I am glad I have not tried rashly to touch it. It would have murdered me as it did that man. It can destroy life just by ordering a man to die! His heartbeat stopped at a telepathic command.

The encephalograph registered the brain's excitement. The pen-stroke was widely deflected, as if the organ moved in its vessel.

I phoned Patrick, but he would not understand. Talking to him was like talking to the brain itself.

If I could produce this explosion of power again, and direct it not against me—that will be my moment! I cannot miss!

I DO not dare take the dead body out of the house, or phone the hospital or the morgue. I am afraid the brain will stop me, and I could not take that risk.

For two nights I have not slept. I do not dare close my eyes for fear of missing the moment. Also the gnawing doubt whether I can succeed is undermining my courage.

Patrick in his admirable intellectual honesty often told me I was a failure. Now I am not so sure that I am. A man sometimes needs a whole life to learn a single truth, and this is the truth and the advice I am leaving.

Don't try to find God in your test tubes, Patrick. Look among people and you will meet Him there!

Here the pages end.

SCHRATT was dead when we arrived in Washington Junction.

Janice and I did not talk about him during our fast journey along the two hundred and fifty miles of highway. We knew what to expect.

She was sitting very close to me so that I should feel the nearness of her body. Every breath she took was to make me aware of her presence. I had only to look into her face, calm in its precognition, and all fear that Donovan might return evaporated.

When we stopped before our house in Washington Junction, Tuttle came running over from the drugstore. He was relieved to see me. He and Phillips had been worried about Schratt. They had just put a call through to the Roosevelt Hotel. Schratt had left my address with Tuttle in case he should not be seen for three days, but had expressly forbidden them to enter the house.

Thanking Tuttle, I sent him back to his store, assuring him I would call in case I needed him. He left reluctantly and stopped half-way across the street to watch me enter my yard.

We walked through the back garden. I dreaded going into the laboratory. To prepare myself for the inevitable shock, I wanted to look through the windows first.

In the driveway stood a new Cadillac coupé, Yocum's, I presumed.

One of the laboratory windows was smashed in, but the curtains were drawn. Light burned inside, and a buzzer sounded continuously.

I unlocked the back door and told Janice to stay outside until I called her. I wanted to spare her a sight which would be pregnant with horror. But she shook her head violently, and pressed my arm. She did not want me to go in alone.

In the small anteroom Yocum was lying, his face turned toward the wall. Schratt must have deposited him there but had not taken time to cover him with a sheet.

156

Schratt lay in the laboratory, his face in a pool of blood. His big head with its sparse white hair was soiled, his heavy hands were holding the brain. He had plunged his fingers deep into the soft gray mass, holding on to it with all his might, as if still afraid it might free itself and continue its putrid life. The glass vessel was broken, the serum splashed over the floor and walls, the electric wires torn from their sockets. Shapeless and prodded with rubber tubes, the brain still looked formidable in its inert mass.

I lifted Schratt up and carried him into my bedroom. There we washed his hands and face.

What had happened was easy to reconstruct:

When Donovan attacked Janice in the Hollywood Hills, Schratt recognized the angry, neurotic deflections of the encephalogram. He knew the brain was busy with a kill again.

He took his chance and jumped at the vessel, tearing it from its electrical connections.

Immediately the brain left Janice and turned against its attacker. In a desperate effort, concentrating all its power on this new enemy, it killed Schratt. But deprived of the serum and pump, it died too.

Schratt's face showed the typical characteristics of death from coronary thrombosis, including the pallor which follows cyanosis. There was a deep cut on his forehead. But where people display anguish in their distorted features, an apprehensive cognizance of impending death, Schratt's face was quiet and happy. He must have died fast.

As I looked at his face, my brain began to reel. I turned, tortured by a sharp pain in my forehead and my eyes. I saw Janice staring at me in fright.

My body began to tremble frantically. I stretched out my hands for help and she quickly stepped toward me.

Before she could reach me I lost consciousness.

JUNE 1

FOR more than five months I had been confined to my bed, suffering from a reaction to the violent strain my brain had been submitted to. Now I am well on my way to recovery.

I am sitting in the hospital garden, in a wheel chair, dictating to Janice.

She is writing a letter to Chloe Barton. I will turn the secret account over to Chloe. I am certain she will look after Sternli, and also fulfill her father's wish to help those poor relatives of Hinds in Reno and Seattle.

Janice showed me a strange newspaper clipping:

Cyril Hinds, condemned to death a few months ago, has been hanged. At the execution, however, the trap did not open. Hinds had to be returned to his cell and the trap mechanism was repaired.

The strange thing happened a second time. The trapdoor stuck. The lever did not respond to the pull of the switch.

Since a man can be hanged only three times, according to an ancient law, the executioner did not want to take any chances. He supported the door with a wooden beam, which at the right moment he pushed away with his foot.

This time Hinds died.

I watched Janice as she read that notice to me. Her forehead furrowed. She tore the clipping into little pieces, looking at me with a wan smile.

I knew what she was thinking: Donovan's unquenchable energy still roams this mortal world. He had tried again to push through his will, to save Hinds from hanging!

Energy cannot be destroyed.

JUNE 2

HIGGINS, the head physician, visited me today to congratulate me on my recovery. I am out of danger. I can leave the hospital any time, he says.

He asked if I was going back to Washington Junction, and when I said no, he sat around for a while, smoking and looking frustrated. I had to laugh and ask him what he wanted.

Reluctantly he again proposed to me Schratt's vacant job at Konapah. The government has ordered him to engage a competent physician who can run a hospital in that barren country, who will supervise the Indian population and educate them in modern hygiene. Higgins is convinced nobody would be better qualified than I.

I was certain he had talked to Janice before he spoke to me.

"Why shouldn't they just get along with snake charms, if they believe in them? Haven't you heard of healings by faith?" I asked Higgins in Schratt's words. Higgins nodded and smiled.

"Of course. I am not against them, if the charms have been sterilized and some potent medicine added!"

I asked him to give me time to think it over, but I was sure I would accept.

JUNE 5

WE have decided to leave for Konapah, but nothing from our old house in Washington Junction will go with us. It was once a custom of the Indians to burn their tents every seven years, to smoke out evil spirits. We will follow their ancient example. Bad thoughts saturate old furniture. The smell of unhappiness clings to it and travels with it to new surroundings. Everything will be new in the shining place the government has built for us in Konapah. Our thoughts, too, will be new ones.

JUNE 10

WE are leaving tomorrow. Before we go I have to purge from my mind my experiment with Donovan's brain.

I did prove that under certain conditions the tissues of a human brain can be kept alive. What else did I gain by the experiment except to demonstrate that the most important achievement, the synthetic creation of mental improvement, is beyond our reach? Nature has set limits which we cannot pass.

The brain's constructive imagination for mechanical devices and chemical exploitations is limitless, but to create kindness, honesty, love, humanity itself must first grow into that shape.

Man can engender what he is himself. Nothing more.